Heart o

by David Cook

Come cheer up, my lads! 'tis to glory we steer,
To add something more to this wonderful year;
To honour we call you, not press you like slaves,
For who are so free as the sons of the waves?

Chorus
Hearts of oak are our ships, heart of oak are our men,
We always are ready: steady, boys, steady!
We'll fight and we'll conquer again and again.

We ne'er see our foes but we wish them to stay,
They never see us but they wish us away;
If they run, why we follow, and run them ashore,
For if they won't fight us, we cannot do more.

Chorus

They swear they'll invade us, these terrible foes,
They frighten our women, our children, and beaus;
But should their flat bottoms in darkness get o'er,
Still Britons they'll find to receive them on shore.

Chorus

We'll still make them fear, and we'll still make them flee,
And drub 'em on shore, as we've drubb'd 'em at sea;
Then cheer up, my lads! with one heart let us sing:
Our soldiers, our sailors, our statesmen and king.

Chorus

'Heart of Oak' was a very popular military song, and to this day is the official march of the United Kingdom's Royal Navy. It was originally written as an opera and sung for the first time in 1760. There is an American version called the 'Liberty Song'.

It was dawn and three longboats approached the northern shore of Gozo.

A frigid wind whipped over the waves. During the night, they had smashed white against the coast, but the storm clouds had gone, torn ragged by a morning gale that had now subsided to a gentle breeze that allowed the boats to cut through the water with relative ease. Behind them, silhouetted and anchored offshore to the west, was HMS *Sea Prince*; a third rate seventy-four gun vessel of the line. The huge square-cut sails, turned dirty white by the long usage of wind and rain, reflected in the sea.

The boats, manned by sailors of His Britannic Majesty's Navy, carried a company of red-coated marines; tough and versatile soldiers, who were led by a man who looked as every bit as hard as they were.

Captain Simon Gamble was twenty-nine years old, and had enlisted at eighteen as a second lieutenant. He was average-looking with a soldier's face; sun-darkened, harsh and scarred. If you were to pass him in the street, you would pay him no attention, but if you saw his sea-blue eyes, then you would see that they sparkled brightly, accentuating his rough exterior to give it an odd gentleness that made him memorable. His scarlet coat and crimson sash were patched and heavily stitched and he was armed with a cutlass, a straight-bladed sword of extraordinary ugliness. It had a rolled iron grip, a thirty-inch blade, and curiously tied to the pommel was a scrap of a tattered silk. It had belonged to his mother; a parting gift for her young son who promised to return home with enough money to pay for his father's grievous arrears that had cost the family their home. A bone-handled dirk and a large pistol were tucked into his belt, which were also hooked to it in case he dropped them overboard during a fight aboard a vessel.

Gamble trained his telescope east to a narrow beach where waves exploded in bursts of foam on the massive limestone rocks. Dim in the gauzy light from the spray that drizzled like fog, he focused on the dark, almost black enemy gun batteries high upon the bluff. He had recently been part of the marine force under the command of Sir Sidney Smith who had helped defeat the French army under General Bonaparte at Acre during the bitter siege. Now he was about to lead his marines up that beach to where, in the half-light, they were to storm a redoubt, and silence those great guns that guarded the great expanse of blue-green Mediterranean Sea. Then, once he was satisfied the redoubt was secured, he would take his men overland to capture a French held fort situated on the Gozo's south-west coast.

The French had seized the Maltese Islands a year before and garrisoned it with over three thousand prime troops. There were many coastal defences, but the local Gozitans and Maltese confirmed that the French garrisons were too few and, encouraged with the news, the British naval taskforce had arrived to blockade the French into submission. The local resistance fighters pledged to support any British land attack.

'How many of the Frogs did you say there were here?' Gamble asked his Maltese guide.

'Fewer than fifty,' Giuseppe Falzon replied softly in his accented English. He was dressed in civilian clothes, but a large blue boat cloak was draped over his shoulders. 'They will be asleep now. They watch the sea, but think any likely attack will come from the south. Over land. They will not suspect a landing here of all places.'

'They'd better not do, Zeppi,' Gamble warned, eyes still fixed on the enemy ship-killers, 'otherwise we're dead men. But we have speed and surprise in our favour, and my marines are the best fighters known to mankind,' he said proudly so the entire boat could hear. He meant every word of the praise. The battles had hardened them like a tempered sword, forged in blistering flame. The men grinned back. The captain switched his stare to the Malteseman. 'However trusting of my rogues to do the task, you know the rules.'

Zeppi sighed as though he was being harangued. 'I know, I know.' He worked for British Intelligence and had first alerted London of the French fleet sailing to the islands, but now on land served as a local guide and would not take part in the attack. 'I'm to stay out of harm's way just like your stinking, flea-bitten dog.'

'Someone has to keep Biter on his damned lead,' Gamble said with a laugh. In truth, Biter, the marines mascot, was still on-board the *Sea Prince*, because it was too risky to have him accompany the landing for fear of him alerting the sentries.

'Biter would love a go at the Frenchies, sir,' said a gruff-voiced sergeant.

'Aye, Sergeant Powell,' Gamble replied, 'but the lads need to earn their pay and I'm not sure King George would approve of Biter doing all the work.'

'In that case, sir,' Powell jutted his unshaven chin at the man next to him, 'Marine Bray should forfeit his entire pay.'

The men roared with laughter at the squirming soldier and Gamble allowed it because laughter counters naked fear, and besides, he thought Bray was the most incompetent man under his command. He was round-shouldered, and resembled a fish with his protuberant eyes and slack mouth.

'That ain't fair, Sergeant,' Bray moaned at the ripple of bawdy laughter.

'Hold your tongue, you useless cur,' Powell scolded, 'or I shall cut it out and feed it to the fishes!'

'Steady, boys! Steady!' Brownrigg, the *Sea Prince*'s boatswain called.

'Here we go,' First Lieutenant Henry Kennedy said, as the boats neared the beach. He was immaculately dressed in his scarlet coat with its long-tails, silver lace, white gloves and a silver gorget.

'Steady! Now!' Brownrigg thumped a calloused hand onto the stern's gunwale, as the water made a sucking noise. All of a sudden, the seamen were overboard, up to their knees in cold water, and expertly dragging the boats toward the shelving beach. 'You lobsters have fun,' he grinned at the nickname given to the marines for their red coat. He was a dark-haired man with a fierce temper. 'Bring back plenty of loot, and that includes any unhappy whores you might find. I'll soon make 'em earn their wage.' He gave a foul smile of small yellow teeth. 'And don't forget to kill the Frog bastards whilst you're there.'

'I certainly won't,' Gamble replied with a curt nod.

As the boats took to the sand, the war-like marines clambered out. They relished the chance for a scrap and, grinning like madmen, were eagerly anticipating the assault. Whetstones had kissed the steel bayonets and their smooth-bore muskets had flint's-re-seated, locks oiled and barrels cleaned out. But Gamble knew most of his men carried dirks. You could fire a musket and pistol once, but a blade kept on coming. The marines were ready for anything.

'Form up,' Powell instructed as quietly as he could, which was a feat because Archibald Powell was stern, loud and could out swear any other man Gamble knew. 'Form up, you heathen sods. Quickly now!' His brusque voice was deepened by years of salt air.

Powell was like an oak, Gamble often reflected; his torso was like a wide-bellied trunk, his arms were like knotted branches and his weathered-face like rutted bark. He bristled with weaponry. 'It puts the fear into the enemy,' the Plymouth-born veteran once said. Powell carried a long-barrelled musketoon; a weapon that had a flared muzzle comparable to a blunderbuss, and recoiled when fired like a small cannon. He also carried a boarding pike with a hook on the reverse side of the blade instead of the regulatory sergeant's halberd. Curiously, he owned a pair of throwing axes, much like a tomahawk, which each had a spike atop the blades head. They had been a gift from a Shawnee Indian named Blue Jacket who had allied with the British during the war against the Americans. A young Private Powell had saved the Indian's life during a skirmish and Blue Jacket had given him the pair in gratitude, an act that had been acted out at almost every campfire and at almost any opportunity.

The marines were armed with Sea Service muskets, blackened to help prevent them from rusting at sea and were carried over shoulders with white slings. They were each equipped with sixty rounds of ball ammunition and bayonets, but at the moment, the weapons were not primed and the blades hung in scabbards at their hips. They were in light order for manoeuvrability, and so their blankets and packs had been left on the *Sea Prince*. Their canteens were full with water, and stored in haversacks was enough hard tack biscuit for a full three days.

Gamble watched all but one of the longboats return back to the ship.

'The lads are in high spirits,' said Kennedy.

'So they should be, Harry,' Gamble said, watching the rocky crest above them with his eye piece, 'they know we're about to do some killing.'

'Won't we take any prisoners, sir?' asked Second Lieutenant Samuel Riding-Smyth, with abhorrence at the thought of killing all of the Frenchmen. He was petrified and fought down vomit, which was souring the back of his throat.

'Oh, Sam,' Kennedy said, shaking his head with an act of despair.

'What happens if they surrender?' Riding-Smyth looked pained.

Gamble grunted in frustration. 'If you want to take any prisoners, then that's your prerogative,' he announced, but was still watching the limestone hills. 'Do you know the Frog word for surrender?'

'*Capitulez*, sir,' suggested the worried lieutenant.

Gamble lowered the brass tube angrily. 'Fine, Sam. You ask any Monsewer you come across to *capitulez*. You shout really loud though, as the buggers will be gunners and we all know that gunners are deaf. You shout and hope they lay down their arms and that they don't meet Sergeant Powell first.'

Riding-Smyth 's eyes slid to the grizzled, broad-shouldered sergeant who stared back at him intently, and for good measure, patted one of his axes with a long exaggerated growl.

'It suits me, sir,' Powell declared. 'The bastards will be easier to kill if they keep nice and still. Saves me the bother.'

'I will shout, sir,' the young officer said zealously. 'I will indeed!'

'Good,' Gamble said, turning to his men who were formed up and waiting with expectant faces. The ball was about to start. It was time to dance. 'Company! Forward!'

'We're not really going to kill all the Frogs, are we?' Kennedy enquired as they advanced up the narrow beach.

'Of course not,' Gamble gave him a sly wink. 'That's why a boat will remain here. I'll send the prisoners back to the Prince of Waves,' he said, giving the *Sea Prince* its nickname, 'along with any keepsakes.'

'Very good,' Kennedy said, then frowned. 'I thought you spoke Frog?'

Gamble scanned the grassy bluffs ahead. 'You mean *Guernésiais*?' he asked, of the language of his native Guernsey that had roots in Norman French. Kennedy nodded. Gamble's mouth twisted. 'I understand the words, but I choose not to speak it. It's the language of our enemies. And I will not foul the air by muttering it.'

'You truly hate them, don't you?'

'I hate them all,' Gamble said loudly. 'As every Englishman should. Death to the French and every goddamn last one of them.'

'I've heard that French is the language of love?' Kennedy said with an impish grin.

Gamble laughed sourly. 'The whores don't care where you're from. Just if you have coin to pay them.'

...*you shall pay life for life*, a voice uttered in Gamble's head. He'd heard the saying many times since Acre. Too many times now. A friend had died and the words kept coming back to him. He adjusted his bicorn and looped the scope over his shoulders with its leather strap, trying to force the words from his mind, but without much success.

'Why don't we turn the prisoners over to the locals, sir?' Riding-Smyth enquired, catching up with his two superiors.

'Because that's a death sentence,' Gamble replied brusquely.

Kennedy fiddled with the gorget at his throat, a purely decorative horseshoe-shaped piece of metal that harked back to the days when officers had worn armour like medieval knights. 'As civilised men, we could not simply allow that to happen. Even to our bitterest enemies. However, knowing that they will be fed whatever Slope the Ship's Cook can boil up in his infernal copper cauldron is punishment and revenge enough.'

Riding-Smyth chuckled. 'At every mess time, I pray to God that He will keep me safe from harm.'

'He must be watching over you,' Kennedy said, 'because as of yet you've not suffered from any of the maladies that frequent the decks.'

'The Lord has truly been kind to me,' Riding-Smyth replied vehemently.

'You've obviously not been introduced to the lower deck whores, young Sam,' Kennedy said wryly. 'When you get back on-board, I'll have a dose of mercury on standby.'

Gamble liked his two subalterns. Harry was twenty-four, a fair and amiable man from Saltash who had been his lieutenant for three years. Sam had spent a little over a month with his new company. He was sixteen, religious, very keen, but had not seen any action. His predecessor, Robert Carstairs, a popular officer, had died fighting French grenadiers at Acre in May, as they attempted to take the entrenchments outside the city's walls. Gamble missed him dearly.

He remembered the smell of death; a sickly, clogging sweetness of putrefaction from the bodies that lay for days under a burning sun and a cold night sky. The stench was unforgettable, and he sniffed thinking he could still smell it now, but he knew he was imagining it. A score of marines had died in the attacks and he himself had been injured; his face still bore the scars from an enemy blade that had lopped off most of his left ear and carved open his jaw. Acre had somehow held out and the French, plague-ridden and bloody, were forced to withdrawal. A coup for the history books, yet achieved at such a dreadful price.

'We're half a mile from the guns, wouldn't you agree?' Gamble asked Zeppi after marching for twenty minutes. He had noticed that his friend was looking solemn and was trying to make conversation.

'Yes,' the dark-haired man replied, 'and this path will soon take us to the hollow where it splits beside the redoubt. From there, you'll be right there under their noses.' He was leading the marines up a sheltered track from the beach, and moved with considerable speed as though he wanted the attack over with.

Gamble understood fear. Every day he woke wondering if it would be his last, and every night said prayers of thanks to whichever deity looked after soldiers.

'Soon be over,' he said confidently.

The hollow was where the company would split into its two platoons. The first under his command would move south to where a watchtower guarded the main road to Rabat, the islands capital. Zeppi had said the tower was a ruin with a long-collapsed stairwell that would offer no defence, and was only used to shelter from winter rains and cold winds. 'It is haunted with the spirit of a girl who was said to have fallen down the steps. No one came to her aid and her ghost walks the ruins. At night, or when the sky is still dark, you can hear her pleading cries for help.'

'We don't have to go inside the tower, do we?' Sergeant Powell, in his mid-forties, with a battered face from numerous tavern and alley brawls, suddenly looked concerned.

'I'll hold your hand if you'd like, Sergeant?' Kennedy feigned mock sympathy.

'I need both hands free for my axes, sir,' Powell growled the reply over the gale of laughter, 'but I thank you for your kindness, nonetheless. Touched by it, I am. Touched.'

'It astounds me how Sergeant Powell can make "sir" sound like a question,' Kennedy said.

'I've noticed it too,' Gamble concurred, 'but it's only when he addresses you.'

The main objective was to secure the road and neutralise the sentries there, and no better job was tasked than to two particular Marines. Mathias Coppinger, half-Danish, and claimed to be a son of 'Cruel Coppinger', an infamous Danish smuggler who terrorized the coasts of Cornwall, and The Dane had inherited his father's unpitying skill with a blade. The second was Nicholas Adams, a slim man with villainous hollow cheeks and quick intelligent eyes that showed little emotion. The company had nicknamed him 'Adder' for his coldness and slender build.

The second platoon under Kennedy would approach the redoubt from the west which overlooked the batteries. By taking his platoon down the road and securing the few buildings, Gamble anticipated the stronghold would be in British hands within minutes. But he had

15

seen enough of battle, of the chaos that descended when musket volleys shattered the air and how the ground tremored when cavalry charged with long blades, to know the simplest plan could go awry in the time it took a man to whisper his sweetheart's name.

The track led the marines above the tumble of sand dunes into the barren coastline, where the wind whipped cold, and Gamble shivered. Strands of sand blew about his feet, but he was glad to be on land, nonetheless. It wasn't the thought of going back to horrid rations where men gave names to the weevils that infested the ship's biscuits, or the boiled salt-meat, or the drinking water which was sometimes slimy. It was the thrill of being on enemy soil, and the impending fight. This was what the marines were trained to do, what they were paid to do, and the boredom of ship life was soon forgotten and replaced with unabated exhilaration.

When Zeppi took them to the basin, the sound of the waves crashing against the rocks dulled to a whisper. It was here the men split into their platoons.

'No heroics, Harry.'

'You know me better than that, sir,' Kennedy shrugged innocently.

The memory of Carstairs' death ran through Gamble's mind again, unbidden, and he clenched his fists against it. He did not want to lose another friend. But Kennedy was already turning away so his eyes flickered to the man to the right of him. 'And that goes for you as well. You do exactly what Harry says.'

Zeppi waved a hand in irritation. 'I'm no babe in need of swaddling,' he answered back, a trifle defensively. 'My countrymen have already rebelled triumphantly and the French cowards scuttled to hide in their forts. I can fight. You know I can!'

Gamble rounded on him, feeling a stab of irritation. 'You are here as our guide and you're no good to me dead. Leave the fighting to my marines.' He knew he had sounded harsh, but it was for his friend's own good.

Zeppi hesitated, then gave a sparkle of understanding before joining the rear ranks of Kennedy's platoon.

Gamble then took his platoon up the ridge. From here, in the distance, the watchtower was a dark silhouette against the rather austere skyline. He could see an orange light flickering at the base of the tower, which betrayed a sentry's fire to ward off the morning's grey chill. The ground dipped with jagged ruts, and was swathed in thick patches of white-flowered Star Jasmine, so it looked as though a blanket of snow had fallen in the night. The sentries walking the walls of the redoubt could not see the marines as they moved southwards below the great cracks of jutting rock. He watched the two chosen men, their red coats, white breeches and black gaiters in stark contrast to the pale foliage, skulk low towards the tower, grasping their wickedly sharp knives. They disappeared and he scratched at the pink scar tissue along his jaw line with a ragged nail, remembering the Frenchman that had cut him at Acre's battlements. He was now dead, but Gamble could still hear his triumphant laugh ringing out, deriding and scornful.

'All clear, sir,' Coppinger whispered when the two men returned shortly. Gamble's nostrils were instantly filled with the stink of fresh blood. He didn't need to know any facts; all he needed to know was that the job was done and the sentries were neutralised. The smirk on The Dane's face and the glint in Adams' eyes - like the scales of a fish just below the waterline - told him that they had enjoyed the killing. Coppinger's white cuffs were stained red.

'Good,' Gamble replied. He swivelled his head to the platoon behind, waving an arm. 'Forward! Forward!' he said in hushed tones.

They moved out like wraiths towards the tower that had been built on a slight rise beside the road, which ran straight to the barracks giving the redcoats a good vantage point. Creeping low, they made their way forward where again Coppinger and Adams hunted ahead. The sound of the waves breaking upon the shore was still muffled. Somewhere nearby a blue rock thrush gave a melodious call. Otherwise it was eerily quiet.

The ground was hard, but with scattered patches of loose scree. Both scouts stopped. Gamble ordered his men to halt and went ahead, keeping low. Hearing a sudden noise like a man's cough, he feared, for a heart's beat, that an unseen sentry was walking up the road towards them. He cast his eyes towards the enemy position and then relaxed. A Frenchman was bringing water from a well near the barrack houses. Gamble moved and dropped flat to count the sentries through his glass. After ten minutes, he counted two on the northern wall. No one else had moved. A wind, lifted off the sea, gusted past and he shivered again. He always considered the Mediterranean islands as hot and dry lands, and so they were in the summer months when the sun burned mercilessly, but in the winter the rains battered the land cold and the wind stabbed like a hunter's spear.

But in truth, he was nervous.

He gazed down at the defences. A single track led to the enemy lines along the neck of land, the sea to the east, where the early morning sun glimmered it gold. There didn't appear to be a gate as such, just a series of platforms that were unmanned. Three batteries faced north, west and east, and he counted a total of nine guns. Four of them looked like big naval beasts. Thirty-six pounders, he reckoned. Beneath the semi-circular wall were several small tiled huts joined together which he concluded were the barracks. He saw a stone well and a ruinous building where four sorry-looking horses that looked like Welsh cobs were stabled. It was a remote redoubt, strangely undermanned in a hostile land. A washing line hung from a window to an araar tree. The tree's thick, leafy branches obscured the roof of the barracks that would offer plenty of shade in the summer. A goat, tethered to one of its low hanging boughs, cropped its head at a tangle of grass. Gamble trained his glass on the western wall and, after a moment of seeing nothing but empty stone, he caught a glimpse of red and white. Kennedy was in place. None of the muskets was loaded. He had insisted on that, fearing an accident which would betray their presence.

Gamble waited a few more minutes and when no enemy sentries threatened, he gave the order to load. When the last man had finished, he waved the marines on down the track.

Now was the time.

Their boots were loud, but no one called out to challenge them. There was no musket discharge, no enemy ball struck his body. No one had seen them.

His muscles were tense and the wind gushed in his ears. He could smell the aroma of bay leaves coming from a laurel bush near the araar. The goat saw the men, watched them approach and bleated softly. His heart hammered in his chest. He didn't know why he was nervous, he'd been in far worse situations. Perhaps each action got harder for the soul to deal with. Gamble would lead his men into the barracks by bayonet point and take sleepy prisoners. He did not expect a fire fight this morning, merely a scuffle and an easy victory borne out of luck. However, he knew that it could also mean death, or of the terrible wounds that prolonged life to that of nightmarish suffering.

But luck was fickle and the enemy saw them.

A sentry on the high northern wall had bent down to light his pipe and had caught sight of the white cross-belts in the shadows of the rocks. He staggered with the discovery and managed to shout out in alarm before a musket banged and he was flung back over the wall and down onto the rocks. The other sentry was more vigilant and took cover behind one of the broad thirty-six pounders. Gamble swore as French voices shouted to gather arms.

'Marines!' he shouted. 'Two lines! Make ready!'

'Two lines now!' Powell said. 'Form up, you lazy bastards!'

What Gamble needed was cohesion. He would form his platoon in two lines inside the redoubt to prevent any enemies trying to escape by the path and also the muskets faced the buildings. From above, Kennedy's platoon would clear the gun batteries and be able to pour fire down onto the square if needed. Gamble, pleased at their positions, hoped the French, seeing that they had nowhere to go, or with little choice to continue, would simply lay down their arms.

The wooden door of the barracks opened and several Frenchmen appeared, some half-naked in shirts, or in breeches and hats, but all with firearms.

Gamble unclipped his pistol, pointed at the door and pulled the trigger. The shot echoed across the courtyard. Moustached faces scowled.

'Lay down your weapons!' he shouted. 'And put your goddamn hands up!'

'*Capitulez*, sir!' Riding-Smyth said encouragingly.

But the French, led by a bearded sergeant, stubbornly refused and a half-dozen enemy muskets went to shoulders. Gamble, half-expecting the refusal, brought his sword down.

'Fire!'

Triggers were pulled, dog-heads snapped forward, flints sparked and set off the powder in the pans which flared and ignited the main charge. The noise and the flame and the burst of smoke were almost simultaneous as the volley blasted out at the Frenchmen.

'Load!' he moved to one side, so he could see through the rising smoke and saw that a dozen of the enemy were already climbing the steps to the batteries. A musket fired from the doorway at the marines, but the ball went high.

'Obstinate bastards, sir!' Powell said admiringly, as a crackle of musketry echoed from the batteries. He scratched a louse bite at one of his thick black side whiskers that framed his battered face.

The front rank loaded with some difficulty as a bayonet-tipped musket was harder to load and knuckles scraped against steel. The wooden ramrods thumped in the barrels. The British Sea Service musket was based on the Land Pattern version that the infantry used, but was notoriously even less accurate, and came equipped with wooden ramrods as steel corrodes in salty air.

'And we know what the Frogs hate the most, don't we?' Gamble said loudly, so that his men could hear.

'Aye, sir,' Powell replied with a lop-sided grin. 'John Bull's cold steel. The Yankees hated the sight of them too.'

More French emerged from the barracks. A loose volley of shots was fired at the marines and miraculously none suffered a scratch. A French bullet slapped Corporal Jasper Forge's black bicorn from his head, leaving him unscathed. Opposite the barracks was a small stone house and at the doorway a tanned officer appeared. His blue jacket was unbuttoned and his face showed that he was utterly shocked at this attack. He shuddered momentarily, like a beast tethered to a slaughtering block, then the realisation hit him, and the officer began to shout commands.

'Charge bayonets!' Gamble shouted. He would take his redcoats close to the enemy now. 'Advance!'

The thirty marines advanced into the courtyard as the French officer tried to rally his small command where there were already eight dead. He knew it was a lost cause for his command was scattered. He stared at the officer commanding the impudent redcoats, wanting to get a good look at his face to see whether he was a gentleman. The multitude of scars, his ugly straight-bladed sword and patched uniform proved unlikely.

'Surrender!' Gamble shouted at him, but his words were drowned out by another volley of musketry coming from the steps and windows.

A ball snatched a marine backwards. Gamble heard a ball hum past his head. He turned just in time to see a French corporal approach the nearest window of the barracks and lunge with a bayonet-tipped musket. Gamble brought his sword up and knocked the blade aside as the Frenchman, snarling with several gold teeth, pulled the trigger. The musket spat angrily, and sent a gout of hot smoke into thin air. Gamble lunged and the heavy cutlass scraped against the corporal's ribs. He let the man fall away onto one of the sleeping cots.

Somewhere a man cried pitifully whilst another gasped and breathed hoarsely like an exhausted animal. The goat was bleating madly and one of the horses had bolted free to entangle the group of French by the steps.

'Lieutenant Riding-Smyth!' Gamble called out.

His subaltern appeared immediately. 'Yes, sir?'

'Take ten men into the barracks and clear the rooms.' He didn't want any enemies threatening his rear. 'Go in with the steel, disarm them, and prod the bastards out like cattle.'

'Yes, sir!' Riding-Smyth blanched, but disappeared with Corporal Tom MacKay's section.

Gamble looked at the remainder of his platoon. 'Advance! At the double!'

The French fired again and a marine fell against the well, hit in the leg. He stood, hobbled a few steps, but then had to steady himself on the masonry for support as bright blood spread on his breeches above the knee. A Frenchman, barefooted, tripped on the araar's roots and as he was getting up, Corporal Forge shot him through the forehead, spattering blood and brain matter over the hanging washing. Marine Frederick Crouch laughed madly. Men slipped on blood or tripped on corpses. Marine William Marsh slammed the butt of his musket into the forehead of a foe, then shot dead another aiming a carbine at Forge.

'I owe you a drink for that, Bill!' the corporal said.

Gamble could sense that this tussle was almost over, could feel it in his instincts, and his blood and bones. He knew they had won. Then, he looked up to see Zeppi fighting desperately. The damned fool! What the hell did he think he was doing?

'Take command, Archie!' his voice boomed across the courtyard. 'Press them hard!' He dashed through the powder-stink of the volleys.

Five Frenchmen had already given up and each one had thrown down their weapons in submission. Two were bent down, hands touching the dusty ground. The officer still at the doorway pulled up a pistol and trained it on the tall marine officer as he surged through the smoke and pulled the trigger. The bullet smacked into the stonework of the barracks. The Frenchman cursed at his haste and saw that the marines were too close so he closed the door and bolted it shut.

Gamble jumped a body killed by the volley, and flicked bayonets away with his sword as he approached the steps. He saw a Frenchman, naked to his waist, aim his musket, but had to trust that the ball would not strike him. He heard a flint strike steel and saw the muzzle flash, but the shot missed him as he ran on. A French gunner tried to kick him in the face, but he let the leg come forward, caught the boot and tugged hard so that the man fell backwards onto the steps, hearing his bare head smack painfully on stone. The man attempted to move, but Gamble kicked him in the face for good measure, and he slid down the steps; jaw hanging loose and obviously broken. A musket exploded, and the flame was enormous because it was so close, and the ball took a chunk out of Gamble's right boot top.

'Zeppi!' Gamble saw Kennedy knock a Frenchman down and kept him prone with the threat of his drawn pistol. 'Harry! I thought you were watching the bastard!'

'I'm sorry,' Harry replied, 'but he just ran ahead without warning.'

His friend had managed to break free of Kennedy's watchful eye and, armed with a long knife, charged with the redcoats when they stormed across gun emplacements. Zeppi watched as a marine and a French soldier tried to bayonet each other, the clash of blades rang like smiths' hammers, and he ran up and plunged his knife into the Frenchman's neck.

'Die! You godless animal!' he hissed like a lit fuse. 'Die!'

Blood trickled from the enemy's mouth as he disengaged to stagger away. Zeppi, driven by hatred, pounced on the dying man to strike again, but an enemy appeared below him and, before he could twist away, a long French bayonet went up through his side. The guide howled and reeled away with hands pressing the wound. He stumbled and fell away. His enemy was a bearded man with an ugly, bony face. Zeppi knew death when he saw it and spat in defiance.

The Frenchman raised his bayonet, but then turned when he saw the Maltese man's eyes flicker past him. A British officer was running straight at him, cutlass gripped in two hands. He swung it with a roar and with such force that the heavy blade cut through the man's beard and neck like a scythe reaping grass. The head tumbled down the sand-strewn steps and the body crumpled to ooze like a broken wineskin.

Kennedy's platoon were still charging down the steps as Gamble reached his friend. Some were herding prisoners, but most of them were in search of plunder while they still had time to look.

'You stupid little bastard!' Gamble said harshly, as he stooped to inspect the bleeding wound. It was not deep, merely and thankfully, and not life-threatening. 'Pace!' he called over the marine who was good with injuries. 'Get your arse over here now!'

'Sir!' Marine Josiah Pace said, giving the barracks a look of sadness as he envisioned himself going back aboard the *Sea Prince* with plugs of tobacco and bulging wineskins. Pace dropped to look at the four-inch cut, spat on a grubby hand and rubbed the blood away. Zeppi let out a whimper and fresh blood flowed immediately.

'You'll need rum for that, or brandy,' Gamble said.

'I don't drink alcohol,' Zeppi replied. His face was spattered with the sergeant's blood. 'I'm a strict Catholic, or have you forgotten?'

Gamble snorted. 'It's not for you to drink! Pace will use it to clean the wound and his needle.'

'Needle?'

'I'll patch it up nicely, sir,' Pace said, grinning. 'You're a lucky bastard, because the Frenchie missed your kidney.'

'Thank God.' Zeppi could not stop himself from making the sign of the cross.

'What were you thinking?' Gamble said to him. 'I goddamn told you to stay at the rear.' The Malteseman just shrugged meekly. 'You nearly got yourself killed. Let Pace get to work. You're in capable hands. Just look at what he did to my ear,' he pulled back his long hair to expose the mutilated organ.

Zeppi gulped and went as white as cartridge paper.

The fight was over; all but one had surrendered. Gamble left his friend under Pace's care as the marines piled captured muskets, and brought out crates, barrels and sacks. They found artillery and engineer equipment such as handspikes, hooks, drag ropes, rammers, buckets, sponges, pickaxes, shovels, spare gun wheels, a few tool boxes and some farriers' kit. Two wagons containing twelve barrels of gunpowder were found underneath a shady white poplar tree. He inspected it to find it damp, fouled by animals and of very poor quality.

He calmly approached the door to the small house. He had brought Sam with him who had procured two cooked chicken legs, a hunk of bread and a basket of boiled eggs. A salty breeze played with the tall weeds that stood in patches around the redoubt.

'Get the bugger out of there,' he said to the boy, biting into a chicken leg.

'Yes, sir,' Riding-Smyth said and cleared his throat. '*Excusez-moi, monsieur. Voulez-vous s'il vous plaît rendre. Merci tellement.*'

'*Non!*' came the muffled reply.

'He said "no", sir,' Riding-Smyth said, meekly.

Gamble sighed. 'Sergeant Powell?'

'Sir!'

'Would you do me the honour please?'

Powell gave a broad smile and in a flash, his hand withdrew an axe and in a blur of handle and steel, the weapon buried itself firmly in the door with an almighty thud.

A moment later, the door unbolted and the officer came out with his hands raised in submission.

'I rather think we've spoiled their day,' Gamble said. The marines grinned back.

It had taken ten minutes of stealth, of fire, of death to take the redoubt. As coffee was brought to him, and he ate his chicken leg for breakfast, he thought that it was not a bad way to start a glorious new day.

Zeppi was stitched and bandaged and, although ordered to rest, was up on his feet and willing to lead the marines onto their next mission. 'My wound is nothing to what has happened to my people. For the sake of Malta, I will continue,' he said, waving his arms theatrically.

Gamble examined the guns which, to his utter surprise, were of poor quality. One was mounted on a hay cart; Powell reckoned it was an Austrian six pounder. The four thirty-six pounders were the only guns mounted on proper carriages. The rest were twelve pounders and looked as though they hadn't been fired for several months. They had certainly not been maintained; the paint was peeling, the barrels were unpolished and filthy, and most of the metal trappings were rusty.

There were dozens of different types of shot. Gamble wanted it all destroyed: powder, shot and the guns spiked. If the French ever returned, they would find it a ruin. The well was filled in with rocks and lengths of broken timber, the powder rolled and tipped into the sea, and the horses scattered to the hills. He did not want to shoot them; he didn't like killing beasts unnecessary. He had once had to shoot a wounded horse and although it whinnied in agony, he was shocked at what he had done. Riding-Smyth had also found crates of good Sicilian wine and the men cursed when Gamble ordered that they be wrecked.

'Throw them over the walls,' he commanded.

'All of them, sir?' Powell was dismayed.

'Every goddamn skin and bottle, Archie. I don't need our boys stewed when they have work to do. Is that clear?'

'As rain, sir,' Powell commented without much conviction.

'We'll get the job done, sir,' Corporal MacKay said in his usual Scottish methodical way.

The twenty-seven prisoners buried their nine killed. The marines had suffered only three wounded, but unable to continue, they were taken back to the boats to see the surgeon. The French were sent back along with the goat, foodstuffs and a handful of good ammunition under a watchful detail of six marines commanded by MacKay.

Two hours after the attack, Gamble took his remaining fifty men south along the main road to Rabat.

'One down,' he said gruffly, 'one bastard to go.'

'Do you think the next one will be as easy, sir?' Riding-Smyth asked, trying to hold his gaze under his captain's steely expression.

He was in awe, for it was said that Gamble had survived more brawls than could be counted. But his exploits were nothing compared to the greatest sea battle in history: the Battle of the Nile. He had boarded one French vessel and the marines had captured it after a hard fought mêlée under the watchful admiration of Rear Admiral Sir Horatio Nelson. The captain was a hero and Second Lieutenant Samuel Riding-Smyth could not shake the worry of death from his mind. His stomach twisted like knots of fire and he wondered, as they marched, whether his famed captain had ever known fear.

'The next one is a proper bastard,' Gamble replied, oblivious to his lieutenant's anxious thoughts. 'It will curdle your blood. Zeppi, tell our young friend here about it.'

The guide flinched inwardly as though the fort was too painful to talk about. 'The captain is quite correct. A real nasty bastard. It's protected by walls, ravelins, batteries, a ditch and glacis. There's only one way in, too.' He looked sorrowfully eastwards to a small fishing village where his father had said the best clams were found on the island. Many years of peace before the wars. 'It was built in my father's lifetime by the Order of St. John. It sits on a hill overlooking the channel. It was to become another Valletta, to replace Rabat as the new city of Gozo and reinforce commerce between the islands. It was never finished and was abandoned to bats, rabbits and lizards.'

'Until the French came,' Kennedy said.

Zeppi nodded. 'Until the French came.'

'What's it called?' Riding-Smyth asked.

'Dominance,' Zeppi said, crossing himself. 'An apt name, yes?'

Riding-Smyth licked nervous lips. 'And we're going to besiege it, sir?' he asked his captain.

Gamble ran his tongue over the front of his teeth. 'We've no time for that, Sam.' He broke into a laugh as though it was a preposterous notion.

Riding-Smyth dutifully began to laugh. 'I apologise for my naivety, sir. Of course, we fifty could not hope to do such a thing.'

'No. No, we're simply going to march up to it and attack it.' Gamble's eyes were bright and hopeful.

Riding-Smyth went white as pipe-clay, his heart hammered against his breastbone. 'March up to it and...?'

'We'll have help, won't we?'

The guide nodded. 'Two hundred men as promised.'

'Where's the rendezvous?' Gamble asked.

Zeppi stretched out his arm beyond the undulating hills to the south, dark with olive groves and crossed with vineyards. 'Not far from here. They will come tonight. They will come to the temples.'

'They say a giantess built it as a place of worship,' Zeppi said to the three officers, marvelling at the crumbling stonework. Firelight flared and danced brief eldritch shadows up the ancient walls and cast strange shapes in the long neglected grasses. 'It's named after her. Ġgantija.'

As far as Gamble could discern, the Ġgantija temples faced south-east, and yet afforded views of Rabat to the west where tiny lights guttered. Somewhere in the gloom to the south was the fort.

It was an hour after dusk and the redcoats had arrived in afternoon sunlight where, beyond a stand of holm oaks and rocks, the temples stood in eerie solitude. Beyond the age-old buildings there was a high plateau of scrubland covered with Common Myrtle - Gamble gave a lop-sided grin because it was the nickname given to one of the whores frequenting the *Sea Prince* - and the wind brought citrus scents from its flowering buds and the ever present salty tang from the ocean.

Gamble had trodden the neglected stone-lined forecourt into the temples northern entrance. The interior walls were made of rough boulders piled on top of each other. Pillars and upright stones had holes bored into them, like the socket for a protective doorpost, but any sign of the gates were long gone. Animal bones, drifted soil and debris littered the ground and large boulders blocked some apses which Gamble suspected held the skeletons of the ancient dead. Feeling a sense of wonder, he stepped over low stone blocks to find a dirt-covered circular hearth.

'There is a horizontal slab there at the back,' Zeppi had said, his voice echoed in the small space. 'I came here once as a boy and found flint knives.'

'Sacrificial?'

'I don't know. But I looked for human bones and found nothing.'

'What about treasure?' Sergeant Powell's voice was loud as he stepped in, the white NCOs knot on his right shoulder made his frame look oddly shaped.

'I'm sorry to tell you that there is nothing here, Sergeant,' Zeppi replied. 'Greedy men have come here hoping to find gold, but I have only ever found a single Roman coin in these hills.'

'I wasn't thinking of myself,' Powell sounded disappointed, then shifted uneasily. 'Just what the lads are asking. If I tell them there's no gold or silver, then they won't go looting the moment my back is turned.'

'If they do that, then they risk the guardian's wrath,' Zeppi warned, shooting Gamble a sly grin.

Powell, who had not seen the smirk, looked alarmed. 'Guardian?'

'Yes,' Zeppi said gravely, 'it is said that even saying its name will anger it. Many looters here have simply vanished without a trace.

An old and dark magic protects these walls. Tread carefully, Sergeant. Tread wisely.'

Powell, eyes wide with terror, quickly disappeared leaving the guide and the officers chortling.

The marines pooled their tea leaves and it bubbled in a cooking cauldron they had taken from the redoubt. Clay pipes were lit. One or two men took advantage of the rest to sleep. Gamble eased back against the wall as the smell lifted his thoughts. It made him think of faraway home. Drinking black coffee on the tiled terrace over-looking the sea. The scents of thyme, rosemary and sage wafting from the herb garden. Sunlight flooding the solar room. Fire crackling on cold evenings. The cobbled streets of St Peter Port that sparkled in the rain. All was peaceful until he overheard two guttural voices nearby spewing vulgarity.

'He says the girl has a pair of tits too big for her dress. Sixteen and hungry for a white man to whet his blade in her,' said the first, hawking and spitting.

'How the hell would he know?' said the other. 'We ain't going to see her. We ain't passing the town, are we, you dribbling dullard?'

'Ain't a town, is it. Just a bunch of mud huts.'

'We ain't going to see her,' said the second man. 'It's a rumour, 'tis all.'

'Maybe,' the first one said, giving a small mad laugh. 'Maybe there would be a chance once the captain's got his back to us for us to go find out.'

'They'll hang you, you oaf.'

Gamble knew exactly who was speaking. Marines Willoughby and Crouch. Both troublesome devils who had been flogged in the past for petty crimes. Bloodybacks, those men were called. He had even struck Willoughby once during the Siege of Acre, where he was found rifling through a dead man's coat rather than be alert at his post.

31

Gamble swivelled his head and spoke loud enough for all of his men to hear, knowing it was nothing more than drink-fuelled gossip.

'One word of trouble from anyone, and I'll kill the man responsible for it. Understand?'

There was silence, broken only by a murmur of obedience. The two men in question gawped for they considered they were safe from his ears. Crouch nodded with agreement, but Willoughby, a hulking man even broader than Powell, offered a defiant smirk, before reluctantly accepting the order with a curt bob of his head.

Gamble looked at them both in the eye.

'Trouble, sir?' Kennedy enquired, sitting down next to him.

Gamble tore his gaze away from them and blew out a lungful of breath. 'No, Harry. Not yet. However, I want those two bastards under close watch.'

'More so than usual, then,' Kennedy gave a cynical smile. 'Willoughby is indeed a troublesome wretch.'

'If I catch him at his tricks again, I'll hang the bastard. And this time no one will stop me.'

He let his eyes fall upon the three freshly caught rabbits roasting over the blazing fire. The smell made his aching belly rumble with hunger. Rabbit stew was Timothy's - his younger brother's - favourite dish. His father's too. Dark gloomy thoughts penetrated his exuberance and a creeping sourness squirmed in his gut. His father had wagered the house and their business and lost it all. He had ruined the family. Law said he was not responsible for any of his father's debts, but Gamble would not have the family name tarnished. They faced penury and another winter where his mother and sisters' future was uncertain. Both brothers vowed to bring back money to reclaim their family estate. If this mission went well, then there was a chance he would return with a sizeable amount of prize money.

'It would taste better with garlic,' Zeppi advised, busily rubbing in salt and sage to give it more flavour. He tested the meat with a knife.

'I can't stand the stuff,' Gamble muttered, still reeling from the bitter thoughts. 'Give me a plate of roast mutton, or beef with potatoes and gravy any day.'

Zeppi shook his head at the captain's lack of culinary adventure. 'Fried rabbit with wine and garlic. Now that's a proper meal,' he said, the whites of his eyes glistening in the flame light.

'I suppose the guardian doesn't mind us lighting a fire, and eating and drinking then?' Gamble said, throwing his friend a wry smile.

'It's fine when it's an islander doing it,' Zeppi replied with a deliberate shrug.

'Have we got any wine?' Kennedy brightened up.

Gamble looked thoughtful for a moment. 'Sergeant Powell?'

'Sir?'

'Have we any wine?'

Powell bit his lip and tried to look innocent. 'Now if only you'd have asked me to keep some back, sir. Instead of destroying them like you instructed, sir. Then you could be enjoying a nice drop of the stuff.'

'Are you saying you didn't keep any?' Gamble asked him, knowing full well that Powell's wooden canteen would be filled with it, as well as those of half of the men.

'You know me, sir. A stickler for orders. Can't abide insubordination.'

'A pity then,' Gamble said in mock disappointment and sighed. 'I'll just have to drink the two I retrieved all to myself then.'

The marines laughed.

'Sir!' A voice called from above.

Gamble looked up to the top of the walls where a marine stood on watch. 'What is it, Nick?'

Adams, the flames accentuating his hollow face and making him appear to be a living skeleton, pointed to the east. 'We've got company.'

The first Gozitans appeared on the track flanked with purple-blue barked tamarisk trees. They were armed with muskets, carbines, pistols and a collection of crude hand weapons: scythes, billhooks, hoes, axes, and staves.

Zeppi went out to meet them. They numbered around forty and they greeted him with curt acknowledgements. Gamble strained to hear their conversation, spoken in quick Maltese.

'They look like keen fellows,' Kennedy muttered.

Gamble looked sceptical.

Apart from the few firearms, the men were nothing more than farmers, fishermen, shepherds, milk-sellers, labourers, and unemployed. The French had dismantled the institutions of the Knights of St. John, an ancient order dating back to the Crusades, including the Roman Catholic Church. Its property had been seized and looted to pay for the French expedition to Egypt, generating blood-bubbling fury amongst the pious islanders. They looked hard, lean and bitter. But anger wouldn't win battles, skill would, and Gamble suspected the Gozitans had never fired a musket in battle before, let alone help assault a fortress. However, deception was the key to this mission's success and the only way in.

'They ain't worth tuppence,' said a voice behind.

Gamble turned to the marines. 'Quiet in the ranks,' he commanded.

The islanders had brought women with them, all dark and slim. They began to build a cooking fire and Gamble suspected they were there to cook for their men rather than be part of the fight. One of them brought over a basket of nectarines, peaches, grapes and cheese made from sheep's milk as a gift. He thanked them for their generosity, trying not to notice the distaste etched on her face at his scars.

'Now that's a rare sight to tighten a man's nuts,' Bray said in wonder, the flame light making his face look uglier than normal.

'Then it's just as well you don't have any,' Coppinger replied.

Adams sniggered, earning a low growl from Bray.

'You want to say something, Adder? I've seen sticks bigger than your arms, you shambling corpse.'

'I've just whetted my knife, Bray. Want to try it out? We want to hear your girlish cries again,' Adams said with a grin. The marines laughed because Bray had been hit in the arm at Acre, a flesh wound, and he had yelped like a girl. The men had not forgotten it.

'Quiet, you ugly whoreson's,' Powell ordered. 'Enough of your coarse chatter when there's pretty ladies present.' The sergeant, never truly comfortable around the other sex, stood to attention, relaxed slightly and then gave the women an awkward bow.

One of the women had vivid green eyes underneath raven-black curls, and gave the officers a wry smile. Kennedy's mouth was lolling open until Gamble noticed and gave him a nudge with his elbow.

'What a strikingly attractive creature,' the lieutenant whispered, gathering a level of coherence.

'Certainly different from what we've been used to.'

'No doubt our men have similar thoughts.'

Gamble glanced at the marines who, starved of regular intercourse, eyed the women hopefully.

'Remember what I said earlier,' he said, loud enough for the ranks at the rear to hear the warning.

There was a buzz of furtive agreement.

Zeppi brought a delicate-looking man with angular cheeks and grey distrustful eyes who scowled at the two lieutenants, and made the sign of the cross at the sight of Gamble's scars. He wore good woollen clothes, a white shirt and reminded Gamble of a stuffy clerk.

'He looks as miserable as a Methodist in a brothel, sir,' Powell said and Gamble smiled.

'This is Baldassar Grech,' Zeppi said, making introductions, and turned to the Gozitan, 'and this is Captain Simon Gamble.'

'Pleased to make your acquaintance,' Gamble offered a hand, the other held a half-devoured peach.

Grech hesitated and then thought better of offending the scarred officer by taking the proffered hand. 'Captain,' he smiled showing small white teeth, but his tone was icy. He rubbed his palms down his sides. 'May I ask which regiment you are from?'

As miserable as a Methodist in a brothel being handed a drink, Gamble said to himself. 'Eighteenth Company, Third Marine Division,' he replied, wiping juice from his chin.

The Gozitan blinked, and then peered at the red-coated soldiers, eyeing them up as though he was a farmer selling cows at the weekday market. 'Marine? You are marines?'

'Yes.'

Grech blew out a lungful of breath. He turned to Zeppi and launched into a frenetic conversation in Maltese, eyes distended with ire.

'Something the matter, Zeppi?' Gamble asked, an eyebrow rose querulously.

Zeppi held up a hand to stop Grech's furious cannonade. 'He expected a full battalion.'

Grech rounded on Gamble. 'A proper regiment,' he said in English and there was a sudden intake of breath among the collective group. The words echoed between the stones.

Gamble suppressed the urge to flatten the man with his fist. 'You'll find that my men can fight on land just as well as any line regiment. They're tough bastards and they're commanded by one too. They can turn an enemy's flank. They've broken French veterans in Acre. They've boarded and captured a French ship during the Battle of the Nile. My marines are worth more than a battalion. I'd have them with me more than any other redcoat.'

Grech glanced at Zeppi who scowled at the offence. The Gozitan rubbed the small beard on his pointed chin. His mouth twitched. 'I apologise, Captain. I meant no insult. It's just that we were promised a full battalion to attack the fort. Not a company.'

'And?'

'Now I doubt now that we can achieve such a task.'

'Nonsense,' Gamble said, chewing on the fruit. 'The plan still goes ahead. You will assist with the attack and my men will take care of the rest. That is what was agreed.'

'Captain, have you read about the Great Siege of Malta?' Grech asked.

Gamble paused to swallow, wondering where the question would go. 'I have,' he replied carefully.

'Then you will realise that the Turks and the French are more alike than you could possibly think.'

'How so?'

'The siege taught the world that a population, thought as nothing more than peasants, could unite in the face of invasion. That they could show courage and honour in desperate times, and dispel the destructiveness of religious hatred. Boys, who had become battle-weary veterans of the Italian campaigns, had sailed here to conquer Malta. But Captain, let me tell you, they have not. Have you heard of Fort St Elmo?'

Gamble stuck his chin out, and threw away the stone. 'I have heard the name,' he said, wondering if Grech was trying to embarrass him by his lack of Maltese historical knowledge.

'The Turkish fleet arrived with men who had conquered the fields of Europe with their scimitars, elite cavalry mounted on giant horses and devil-men who wore the skins of beasts. Their artillery numbered hundreds and they battered the fort's walls for days. Inside were Knights of St. John. And amidst that hell-fire they refused to surrender. Wave upon wave of screaming Turks tried to capture the breaches, but the defenders repelled them all. They fought with pikes, swords, axes, blocks of stone, and their bare hands. The siege gave the Knights inspiration to invent new weapons: fire-hoops; wooden rings, wrapped in layers of cotton, flax, brandy, gunpowder, turpentine, and ignited and rolled to the enemy. Trumps; hollow metal tubes filled with flammable sulphur resin and linseed oil; and when lit, they blasted flame like dragon's breath. Many Turks with their flowing robes died from these new weapons. For thirty days, the Knights held out. Eventually, they claimed their prize. But the Turks turned to Valletta and committed an utterly despicable act which angered God. They mutilated the fort's defenders, stuck their heads on pikes and floated the decapitated bodies of their officers across the harbour on wooden crosses. It was designed to cause distress and it would have, had it not been for God turning the tide.'

'God?' Gamble said, raising an eyebrow.

'Yes, Captain. God,' Grech insisted scornfully. 'The sun burned like a furnace, and it was said the dead left unburied in the fort blackened and burst, spreading disease to the Turkish camp. They tried to take the city, but the defenders out-thought and out-fought them. God had blessed them with plenty of supplies and ammunition. Even when autumn winds brought rain the defenders muskets and pistols still felled the Muslim attackers. Then a relief force from Scilly smashed the Turks aside. They were pursued across the island, dying in droves at the hands of my vengeful ancestors. It is said the waters of St Paul's Bay turned blood red. The Knights won. Malta was saved.'

'God,' Gamble said again, this time sounding distant.

Grech's eyes narrowed. 'Am I to believe that you are not a Christian?'

'I believe in a good musket,' Gamble replied flatly, irritation creeping back into his voice. 'I believe in the British Navy. I believe in wiping the earth of the bastard French.'

Grech grimaced. 'I see,' his grey eyes flashed at Zeppi, before turning back. 'We have been sent one company of men. Godless men at that, I might add, to do a battalion's job.' He rubbed the ends of his beard with long fingers as though he contemplated his next move.

'Godless men who'll free your country,' Gamble said with a menacing glare. 'What were you trying to tell me with your story?'

'I want to see the French defeated,' Grech said. 'I want our people free. I want the world to see our victory as a beacon for Christianity.'

'You're doing this for God?'

'Yes,' Grech said piously, 'and so should you.'

Gamble shook his head, momentarily confused. 'No, I'm doing this because I've been ordered here by my superiors.'

The Gozitans mouth tightened to a smile. 'And just who do you think told them to send you here?'

The French, Grech explained, sent an armed convoy every two weeks to the redoubt via Rabat to acquire more supplies. He made a crude sketch of the island in the soil with his sword showing the fort, Rabat, the outer villages and the roads. Gamble noticed that the blade was spotted with rust. 'They do buy flour, smoked fish, grapes and local cheese, but there is never enough food for them. There is not enough food for the islanders, let alone the bloody French.' The curse sounded awkward, as though he was not used accustomed to it.

'How many in the fort?' Gamble was making mental notes.

'It is said five hundred,' Grech answered, 'but I believe more likely three.'

'That's still quite a number to hold the place,' Kennedy said.

'Two months ago they sent several boat loads of men to Valletta,' Zeppi said.

'Why?' Gamble asked.

'Supplies?' Kennedy suggested with a shrug.

Zeppi wiped the ends of his moustache with the back of a hand. 'A sickness struck the fort.'

Gamble's eyes bored into his. 'What sort of sickness? I'm not sending my men in if the Toads have got themselves the pox.'

'No,' Zeppi's head shook fervidly, 'nothing like that. A sweating sickness. Perhaps fifty were sent to the *Santa Infermeria*, the main hospital in Valletta to recuperate. I heard from a fisherman that about six weeks after the French took the fort some of their men became sick. There must have been something in the wells. Some foulness. Probably the Gozitans had been pissing in it,' he said, translating it for the islanders who couldn't speak English, who laughed.

'It's a cursed place,' Grech murmured. 'It brings bad luck.'

'That's good for us,' Kennedy put in. 'We don't want to live there. We just want to expel the Frogs. You can have it back afterwards, old boy.'

Grech didn't know if he was being mocked or not, so stared back at the drawing instead.

'So the French supply force will be on the road tomorrow?' Gamble asked.

'Yes.' Grech's gaze trained up to the eastern side of the island. 'They always go along that road and then follow it to Rabat.'

'Why?'

'I understand the French bathe at the beach there,' Grech explained.

'What?' Gamble laughed mockingly.

'The islanders say that the salt water in this particular cove cures all illnesses and so the French make trips there.'

Gamble shook his head, incredulous. 'And I thought I'd heard everything there is to hear.' He chuckled again. 'We're at war and the Frogs want to go bathing.'

'Will we get time for that, sir?' Riding-Smyth enquired.

'No, we bloody won't,' Gamble snorted. 'Our job is to take the fort and hold it until reinforcements come, not to frolic in the waves like bloody mermaids.'

'That's a shame, Captain, because you do stink,' Grech said, tugging his nostrils.

Gamble's eyes devoured the man, taking in his proud and scornful demeanour. 'I probably do stink, but when you were still fast asleep this morning, I was capturing an enemy stronghold.'

'Captain, I ⁻ ' Grech began, but Gamble interrupted.

'I am a soldier and I have seen some truly ungodly things in my life. I've even committed some of them. What you need are men like me to do the job whether I stink or not.'

Grech pursed his lips, not willing to continue the conversation, but enough to have his say. 'Bathing in salt water is good for you,' he muttered, his nose still puckered.

'How many Frogs will there be on the supply run?' Kennedy said. He spoke in the confident tones of a man willing to change the subject to avoid confrontation.

'Usually fifty, Lieutenant,' Grech said. 'Sometimes more, sometimes less.'

'Cavalry?' Riding-Smyth asked.

'No, the French do not have any cavalry on the islands.'

'They have pack horses, of course,' Zeppi added. He peered at the dark hills. 'We've hard soil here and some small patches of woodland, so it is ideal for mounted troops, but they took all their good horses to Egypt.'

'Good for us then,' Riding-Smyth said.

'So after we attack their men out gathering supplies,' Kennedy said, 'what do we do then? The Frogs will no doubt hear the musketry. Won't they send out men to scout the hills?'

'No,' Gamble said, spitting out the end of a broken fingernail, 'because when we ambush the bastards, half of them will be in the sea and the others will be dozing in the sun.'

'They go fishing in the cove too,' Grech added and the marines laughed.

'There you go then,' Gamble grinned like a wolf smelling prey. 'This will be easier than catching crabs in a barrel.'

'If you say so, Captain,' Grech said dubiously.

It would be easy, Gamble added to himself, if Grech and his men don't bugger this up.

Fog wreathed the walls of the temples, utterly obscuring the low courtyard and apses where Gamble, at daybreak, paraded his men.

'Another warm welcome,' Kennedy said sourly. 'That fellow Grech is as sharp as a newly honed blade.' The Gozitans had gone on to drum up volunteers to assist with the attack and would meet at sundown.

Gamble gave his opinion of the Gozitan in the shortest term, which made his first lieutenant smile. 'The islanders doubt they really need us. Their Maltese cousins have already taken all the forts on Malta. As far as they are concerned we're turning up late to the dance as they'll no doubt force the Frogs to surrender anyway. Besides,' he conceded, 'they are none too fond of soldiers, even their allies.'

'That's a shame,' Kennedy brushed at his coat with a gloved hand. 'I have gone to all that trouble of looking so dashing for them.'

Gamble drew and let his cutlass slip home. 'All present and correct, Sergeant?'

'Yes, sir!' Powell replied.

'Then, let's go hunting.'

Their boots crunched and thudded on the road as they marched east into the morning's cold whiteness of the fog. Gamble sent Adams and Coppinger to scout ahead, both men could cross open ground like ghosts. The waylay was less than a half day's march away, but he wanted his men into position long before the enemy got to the cove. The chilliness brought out the pungent smell of wild sage that littered the plateau. There were no rivers or streams on the island, so they followed the road and hoped Grech's information was correct. Another morning's chaos and then after signalling to the *Sea Prince* for reinforcements, they would start their bold attack on Dominance. The French wouldn't even know the marines had landed.

But Gamble thought that he should be the happiest man under the aegis of the Admiralty, for he had been given a land command to give the French revolutionary rats a damned good thrashing. A command to carry cutlass and musket to reclaim a country back from a hated enemy. He was given the freedom to do that; no shackles to hinder. He could fight his own war and take his men into the annals of triumph.

The redcoats climbed a steep hill; the soft fog clung to their salt-stained coats as if they were amongst the clouds. Somewhere off gulls cried, but nothing stirred. It was difficult to see anything; the fog partially concealed the road itself, thick tendrils seemed to grasp at the men's boots as they marched. Their heads were held high because of the black leather stock clasped around their neck which dug into the soft flesh under the jaw. Gamble remembered that Bray had been flogged once because he had been soaping his to make it softer.

He noticed his second lieutenant was struggling with the march. 'Boots giving you blisters, Sam?'

'Yes, sir.'

'You'll get used to it. Your feet will get harder. Aye, it's not good advice, but it's because you're a marine and we don't go on marches. I'll wager that you're looking forward to being back on board, yes?'

'Not really, sir,' Riding-Smyth winced. 'I get terrible seasickness.'

Kennedy laughed loudly. 'What? My dear fellow, you are in the wars.'

'I'd much rather be on land,' Riding-Smyth established quickly, not wanting to appear completely hopeless. He had heard that Nelson suffered badly from it, but the great man could shake it off easily. Riding-Smyth tried to think of that when he was puking his guts out over the side. 'I often went out on hunts with my father and eldest brother. We'd ride for hours and sometimes with our gamekeeper, we'd be out for miles with our fowling pieces in all weather.'

'Are you close to your father, Sam?' Gamble asked.

'Not really, sir. My family owns five hundred acres of fertile land around Tavistock and I purchased my commission rather than follow my father's wishes to manage the farm estates which does not interest me one bit.'

'I bet you're popular,' Kennedy mused.

'He hasn't spoken to me since,' Riding-Smyth said, cheerfully.

'They can ruin lives,' Gamble said. The agonising thoughts of his own father's betrayal and loss of everything they had once known didn't keep plaguing his mind. He chewed the inside of his cheeks, deep in thought.

'Very true, sir,' Riding-Smyth said. 'But the one piece of advice he gave me I ignored much to my chagrin. I should have invested in a pair of decent leather boots.'

'That's the secret to a trouble-free life, Sam,' Kennedy said in his usual amiable tone.

'My cousin is a cobbler, young man,' Zeppi said, 'and he will fix them for a good price. He is very skilled.'

Riding-Smyth's face brightened. 'Really?'

'Yes, he will make your boots feel like you are walking on air. No more blisters. No more pain.'

'Where does your cousin live?'

'Valletta,' Zeppi said. 'If you survive this island, then I would think your next command will be to take the capital.'

'I see,' Riding-Smyth said, shoulders sagging slightly.

'So it's a new pair of boots or a coffin,' Kennedy teased. 'A hard choice.'

The march was warming the men. By nine o'clock the air had become humid and heavy, and the marines sweated in their woollen coats. They had reached the east coast where fishing boats dotted the sea and where clouds sailed like smoky trails. Gamble halted his company and took in the crisp scents of the ocean.

'Does anyone live there?' He jutted his chin to the thin stretch of land situated in the angry iron-grey channel between Gozo and Malta, the latter an imposing block of jagged rock.

'A few hermits,' Zeppi shrugged.

'What's it called?'

'Comino. Named after the cumin plant that is found there.'

Gamble didn't know what that was, and turned his attention to the stone fort, visible above the limestone cliffs dotted with caves. The sea bashed white, sending spray high into the air. 'What's that keep?'

'St Mary's tower,' Zeppi replied. 'It was built long ago by a Grand Master of the Knights of Malta.'

`Do the French hold it now?'

'No, it is long abandoned. I've been there. You'd need a regiment of sappers for a full month to clear it of debris and to shore up the walls. There are some other ruins to the south and a stone church. The Romans had once farmed the island. It was once a prison for traitors, and it has seen its fair share of pirates and smugglers over the years. I heard many tales as a boy. I wanted to be a pirate,' he said with a grin. 'It is now a desolate place, but Comino has a quiet beauty. It is peaceful. I like it there.'

'You like it, because there are no foreigners there,' Gamble needled.

Zeppi smiled. 'Baldassar would agree with that. Although, as I'm Maltese, he's not keen to see me here either.'

Gamble knew of Gozo and Malta's fragile and sometimes volatile alliance. He turned to see two men walking across the dark vineyards to the south. To the east was a small farm where a woman hung out her washing between two trees. A boy played with his dog. The marines remained unseen. It seemed somehow incredible that they could be here with the redoubt taken and no enemy aware of their existence. In Gamble's opinion, the Navy had made this all possible. Nelson was Lord of the Seas and the Royal Navy's 'wooden walls', ruled the waves. After inflicting the crushing victory at the Battle of the Nile, the French had virtually no ships to transport a company of troops into British territory. British landing parties could strike anywhere they wanted and would be gone before the French could bring reinforcements.

'How far until we reach the cove?'

'We'll be there in less than two hours.'

'And the damned Frogs?'

'They'll be there before mid-day,' Zeppi said, holding his wound.

'Will you be all right?'

46

The Malteseman nodded. 'Yes.' He looked down at the road, before looking up to Gamble. 'It was my fault back there.'

'Yes, it was.' Gamble was serious, but concerned.

Zeppi took a sip of water and shook his head humbly. 'I was stupid. I should have listened to you.'

'There might not be a next time.'

'I couldn't stop myself. The French have murdered, stolen, lied and cheated. I hate them. As soon as I saw them I became so angry.'

Gamble clasped his shoulder in friendship, a decade old bond, made in St Peter Port when Zeppi had worked for his father's merchant company. 'Just do as you're goddamn told next time,' he said. 'I promise I'll make them pay. Leave the killing to me.'

'Sir!' Coppinger interrupted.

Gamble turned to stare over the rocky basin. Figures moved on the nearby hills.

'Horsemen, sir!'

'I see them! Everyone get down here! Now!'

The marines scrambled across the roadside and capered to where an ancient carob tree sprouted over a natural spring, an opening deep down in the rocks.

Sergeant Powell thumped a slacking marine into place with his pike before jumping down into the gap.

Gamble rested his spyglass against the rocks to steady the cumbersome device. His view was one of blurred hills, and he twisted the lens until the vision was clear. Four horsemen were walking, rather than riding their mounts, and perhaps forty men - a company - marched in front of a cart drawn by two oxen. They were heading towards the redcoats.

'Looks like the scoundrels happen to be early, sir,' Kennedy whispered ironically, although the French were still half a mile away and could not possibly hear a conversation.

'They are in a hurry to bathe,' Zeppi suggested with a shrug. 'Perhaps they stink worse than you?'

Gamble was deciding what to do. He would spring an ambush on the roadside, but all of his men were now hunkered down on one side of the road. Perhaps there was another way? He beckoned Kennedy to follow him where the land edged down to the sea cliffs. He gestured up at a shadowed depression in the rocks where twenty men could hide from the road above. If he could position twenty marines there and line the road with the rest to block it, then as the French formed up, the concealed marines might spring up and turn the enemy flank to red ruin.

He doubled back with his lieutenant. 'Harry, you see that tumble of yellow grass edging the road?'

'Yes, sir.'

'Take twenty of your platoon down to the hollow and wait for my signal. By my reckoning that is forty yards away. We let the bastards come close and we'll hammer them on two fronts. It will be like boarding a vessel.'

'Yes, sir,' Kennedy replied. 'What about the officers? I'm told that when facing horsemen you should hit the beast rather than the rider.'

'Who told you that?' Gamble grimaced. 'There are only four riders and I doubt they'll give us any trouble.'

The marines waited.

Gamble watched the enemy move inexorably closer. The mounted men were officers and their horses were skin and bone. They wore swords and blue coats, their faces dark underneath bicorn hats. The men were *chasseurs*, light infantry troops, dressed in mostly blue coats and trousers with olive green fringed epaulettes and white cross-belts. They carried a short sabre as well as their musket and bayonet. Coming closer, he could see that their uniforms were patched in a variety of drab coloured cloth. They sauntered rather than marched and he thought they looked like street beggars rather than prime infantry that had shattered the armies of royal Europe. Fighting in pairs, using cover and keeping no rigid formation, the light infantry had sniped at the enemy lines, eating away at them slowly until they had collapsed under the nerve-destroying French artillery, infantry and cavalry support. It was a simple plan and the French were masters of the battlefields.

Two of the officers spurred ahead of the convoy, doubtless wanting to reach the cove where sea bream, squid and whiting could be caught by the barrel load. Curiously, one wore a cavalry cap: a mirliton, and a dolman jacket, and Gamble wondered if the man was a Hussar. Zeppi had said there were no cavalry on the islands because they had all been sent to Egypt with the rest of the Army of the Orient. The officer kicked his mount forward and the other one did the same, and Gamble cursed because they would spring the trap too early.

'Archie!'

'Sir?' Sergeant Powell answered.

'Deal with the bastards, but only if they spot us.'

'Aye, sir,' he said, pulling free his axes. 'Reminds me of the time when I fought the Yankees on detachment duties at the Battle of Oriskany.'

'Not now, Archie.'

The two riders were past Kennedy's group, kicking up clouds of dirty-white dust, and so far the marines remained unseen. Gamble grinned. This would be easy. The *chasseurs* were now approaching a dip in the road and this was the chance of victory. The first rider looked straight into his eyes. He stared fleetingly, until the realisation hit him like a musket ball, and he opened his mouth in warning.

Sergeant Powell drew his right arm back and, in a flash of steel, the blade buried itself in the blue-coated rider's chest with an explosive grunt. The force of the blow knocked the man backwards in the saddle, nerveless hands releasing the leather reins. His eyes were wide in shock and blood trickled from his mouth as he swayed. The mirliton wearing one froze. His mouth went slack. He jerked free his sabre and went to raise it when Adams sprang up and plunged a dirk between his ribs. The marine twisted the blade and hauled on the reins to take the beast off the road. The horseman slumped to the side, hands lifeless, but sword still suspended from the strap around his wrist. Gamble climbed the bank and dragged the dying officer out of sight. Coppinger went to reach the other horse, but it panicked, kicked its hind legs, and reared. The Dane stepped back from its thrashing hooves. The dead officer fell from the saddle, but his boot caught in the stirrup and the corpse was towed behind the bounding horse as it galloped north towards the coast. Gamble watched the body slam into rocks, crunching bone and gashing flesh, until finally the boot unclasped itself and the body lay in a crumpled pile. It was hidden from the advancing *chasseurs* who had neither seen, nor heard the commotion.

The horse that Adams had brought down whinnied loudly and Gamble twisted from the Frenchman who had died. 'Keep that bloody horse quiet!' he hissed. Coppinger and Powell ran to the beast to soothe it. Gamble turned to the others. 'Stop gawking and eyes front! Resume your places!' He saw that the convoy had reached the grass. Now was the time. He stood so that all could see him. 'Form line! At the double! Advance!'

The Malteseman stepped forward and Gamble shoved him back. 'You stay here, you bastard.'

The redcoats scrambled up the bank to form two lines across the roadside. The horse screamed and Powell flailed at the reins. Gamble cupped a hand to his mouth. 'Leave the bloody thing, Archie! Close ranks!'

The *chasseurs* halted and stared with sudden confusion. Then, the officers and sergeants shouted for them to form up. The two-wheeled cart kept moving until the driver hauled on the beast's yokes.

'Get ready to spill some Frog blood, boys! Remember Acre! Forward!' Gamble bellowed. 'Hold your fire!' He wanted his men to be fully-loaded. He withdrew his cutlass. The two remaining horsemen looked like veterans of the wars, hard-faced with a grim confidence, but he wanted the French to fear his men. The two lines of marines walked calmly, and one or two *chasseurs* broke ranks in terror. So far, the enemy had not seen Kennedy's platoon, only to stand and fix bayonets. Gamble noticed some did not have any. 'Halt!' They were a scant fifty yards from the enemy. One of the officers waved his sword about his head as though impatient with his men's discipline. 'Make ready! Present! Aim! Fire!'

The platoon's muskets split the morning air with a sound like the dull tearing of heavy cloth.

'Load!' Sergeant Powell shouted over the din, musketoon slung over his back, and boarding pike in his hands. Sam, who had seen a score of men collapse from the volley, punched the bitter smoke-wreathed air with his sword in triumph and narrowly missed slicing open Corporal Forge's neck.

A marine fumbled his ramrod and received a customary berating from Forge who had witnessed the slip. 'Bray! I saw that! You useless blundering bastard! Pick it up now! You dare show His Majesty's enemy that mistake again, and I'll have you on a charge!'

The *chasseurs*, perhaps half their number as they were still trying to form into line, shouldered muskets and Gamble held his breath. The crackle of shots smashed out, the thrum deafened and the heavy butts leaped back into shoulders. A ball nicked a large stone in front of him. A musket exploded with flame somewhere next to him and he thought the man had fired without permission. A marine, hit in the abdomen, fell sideways and slid down the embankment. He did not move again. Another hit in the throat tried to ignore the wound, but he dropped his musket and fell backwards. Forge dragged him free from entangling the others.

'Close up!' Sergeant Powell shouted, then seeing a marine in the second rank trying to break free, he clasped him by the collar.

Crouch, hissing like a cat, held his right hand with his left. 'A ball has taken a finger away, Sergeant! And it's dented the breech! She won't fire!' He showed the wound and the damaged musket. Powell looked away, stooped and thrust him a dead marine's weapon.

'Now back to your file!' Powell pushed him into position, and patting his shoulder. 'Your trigger finger still works!'

'Take Aim! Aim low!' Gamble shouted.

He had seen the enemy line shudder. British muskets were larger-calibre than the French, and the lead balls lost shape impacting flesh. They smashed apart bone as they drove deep into the bodies. The rear ranks were being pushed into positions over their dead, dying and wounded by the sergeants. One man, lying on his back, was screaming like a vixen. Muskets tipped up as they began to load.

'Fire!' Gamble yelled and the muskets erupted in dirty smoke and the rank smell of black powder. It was another quick, violent, horrifying volley at lethally short range and the curses of the French were wiped into instant silence, or rather changed into screams and sobs.

'Reload! Don't waste your powder!' Powell shouted.

The marines fought on. They did what they were trained to do, and what they did was learn how to fire a musket. Load and fire, load and fire. Months of drill. Pull free a cartridge, bite the top off, prime the lock with a pinch of black powder from the bitten end, close the frizzen to keep the pinch in place, drop the butt, pour in the rest down the blackened barrel, thrust the paper down as wadding, ram it down hard, and inside was the lead ball. Bring the musket back up, pull back the cock, aim, and pull the trigger. Repeat. Mouths would dry out from the saltpetre. Tongues would swell.

Faces and hands would blacken. Eyes would sting from the stink and ears would ring from the roar.

Gamble waited until the time was right. 'Now, Harry! Now!' he roared.

Lieutenant Kennedy's battle-forged men stormed up the verge, screaming like banshees eager for blood.

'*Tirez!*'

The *chasseur* line exploded, but because they had seen and heard a new enemy, it was slapdash as files twisted to face the threat. Bullets whipped the air and two marines of Gamble's platoon buckled onto the stony road. One moved and the other did not.

'Fire!' Gamble slashed the air with his cutlass and the torrent of balls slammed into the French ranks that were in the process of loading, or turning to face Kennedy's men. 'Cease loading!' he yelled, not wanting his men to fire in case they hit their comrades.

Kennedy knocked aside bayonets with his sword and stepped back as a large Frenchman wearing gold rings in his ears lunged with his blade. The lieutenant parried and brought up his pistol to the man's temple. The enemy glared with terrified eyes as Kennedy pulled the trigger and the ball plunged into his skull, erupting from the other side leaving a hole the size of a saucer, and spraying gore over the man beside him.

One of the mounted officers spurred his horse towards Kennedy, beating aside heads with the flat of his epée. He slashed it hard across the face of one marine, taking an eye and the best part of his cheek, brought it up and chopped down through the bicorn of another. He wrenched his arm back, to find the hat was stuck to the blood-dripping blade, and went to hack again when a musket ball shattered his arm. Hands reached up and pulled him from his mount. He fell to the ground, where feet kicked him and bayonets thumped into his writhing body, ripping his flesh and saturating the cold ground with his hot blood. A *chasseur*, belly torn open lay screaming as men trod and slipped on his spilled guts. A knot of Frenchmen broke from their company to fire as skirmishers as they had been trained to do at Gamble's platoon. Their ragged flurry of shots threw one of his men down in a welter of blood.

Gamble, ignoring the small group, looked at his steel-tipped marines. 'Charge bayonets!'

The French company had not reacted well and now the rest of the red-coated enemy charged with muskets tipped with long bayonets as though they were taking an enemy vessel. If the enemy held, Gamble knew, he would lose a good number of men. It was a risk, but one that his gut told him to take.

'For God and King George!' Riding-Smyth chanted, sword held low just as his captain had shown him.

The French gawked through the rank musket smoke, saw the enemy come and broke. Some were too slow and the marines' spikes caught them. Others threw down their weapons and pleaded for quarter.

'Surrender!' Kennedy shouted, eyes blazed through his crimson-spattered face.

'Hands up!' Gamble snarled at one stubborn *chasseur*. He punched him in the face and kicked him down onto the ground. 'Get your bloody hands in the air!'

Powell jabbed his pike lightly at the throat of the last officer. 'Get off your nag, sir! There's a good fellow!' Sunlight reflected brightly on the weapon's tip.

The Frenchman, a captain, knowing he was beaten, cursed and shouted for his men to yield. He kicked his feet out of the stirrups, jumped down and offered his sabre to Gamble.

Gamble gawked, sizing him up. The Frenchman had brown almond-shaped eyes set over a hooked nose, and a strong-boned face. 'Sam?'

'Sir!' Riding-Smyth panted.

'Tell the Crapaud he can keep his blade,' Gamble said and, as the lieutenant relayed the message, albeit slightly altered for politeness, he turned to his men who were still forcing the French off the road. He heard a scream and pushed Sam aside. Two prisoners were crying out as a marine continued to bayonet them savagely. 'Cease that now!' he bawled. 'Marine! Cease what you are doing!'

'You bastards!' The marine was saying over and over, flicking the reddened blade and jabbing it hard. 'Bastards!'

'Cease!' Gamble ordered and was ignored. He tugged the redcoat away with so much force that the man fell to the ground. It was Crouch. His face was twisted into a thing of madness. The French captain jostled his way over with Sam and Harry. Gamble knelt down to the dying *chasseurs*, but there was nothing anyone could do.

The officer exploded in rage, his mouth a misshapen pit of resentment and anger. He spat at Gamble, who was taking the anger calmly. He sympathised, he would have done the same had it been his men who had been butchered. Sergeant Powell brought the pike up to keep the Frenchman back, but Gamble ordered him to lower it.

'Would you like me to translate, sir?' Riding-Smyth asked, hesitantly, but Gamble shook his head.

'I understand,' he said to the Frenchman, feeling sweat bead between his shoulder blades and slicken his palms. 'I will deal with my man accordingly. You have my word as a British officer.'

The captain stared into Gamble's eyes, made hard and almost cruel from the clash. He was still looking intently at him when he spoke.

The young Marine lieutenant looked grave at the Frenchman's hurried reply. 'He said his men were surrendering. They were murdered and . . .' he hesitated, 'he said you may not look like a gentleman, but there must be honour in war. Honour demands punishment.'

Gamble took a deep breath. He glanced at the mutilated corpses and let his eyes roam to the faces of his men; seeing resentment, guilt, triumph, weariness and horror. Crouch, who had his face in his hands, sobbed and babbled wildly.

'I apologise. I give you my word that he will be reprimanded.'

A marine burst through the gaping ranks. 'They weren't surrendering, sir!' Willoughby said. 'I saw it happen. They attacked him and he had to put them down.'

Gamble's temper flared and he reached out and grabbed the hulking soldier by the throat, bristles like a wire-brush dug into his fingers. 'You speak to me again without permission and I'll tear your tongue out of your goddamn mouth!' He hauled him up and pushed him backwards towards Powell who tripped him over.

'Marine Willoughby, you are on a charge! You beef-witted bastard! On your feet!' Powell kicked his heels hard. 'Get up, or I'll knock your bloody ears off and you'll be picking the sand out of them for the rest of the month!'

Riding-Smyth was translating this to the captain who still seethed. He stepped forward and said something to Gamble who told the Frenchman to keep his bloody mouth still. He looked back at the roadside that was splashed with blood, littered with burnt wadding and spent balls. Corporal Forge herded prisoners with his bayonet towards the press of men.

It had taken ten minutes of fire, blade, blood and sweat. The marines had won and their prisoners now sat under guard.

To the south, Fort Dominance guarded the island with its batteries of guns like a watchful sentinel, and whether God wanted it or not, it was where Gamble would take his redcoats.

'Four dead,' Kennedy read out the butcher's bill of names. 'Four wounded. Two severely, the other two have asked to stay.'

Gamble rubbed his eyes as though he was tired. 'Thank you, Harry. Tell the men they did well. Very well.'

Kennedy hesitated. 'I think it would come better from you, sir. After all, they won this fight for you.'

'It's because I mentioned Acre.'

'Aye.'

Gamble smiled. 'I will, but I'm getting a 'there's something else, sir', kind of feeling?'

Kennedy smiled knowingly. 'The lads also want to know what you're going to do with Crouch.'

'It doesn't concern them.'

'I know.'

'He deserves to be shot.' Gamble stared at his lieutenant who was biting his lip. 'What, Harry? What is it?'

'I don't know whether Crouch is guilty. I didn't see what he was accused of doing. He's a dolt and he's been a troublemaker in the past I grant you. But he's one of the more useful of our men. Even with one finger less. Certainly more so than, Uriah Bray,' he said condescendingly.

'I've seen barnacles prime a musket better than Bray,' Gamble said to which Kennedy chortled. 'I've seen seaweed with more intelligence. But where Bray is goddamn useless, Crouch is a vicious little shit. Both him and Willoughby.' *It was a pity they still lived*, he said to himself. They had survived Acre, and the Nile when other men, good men, had died. An image of Bob Carstairs flashed in his mind's eye. The lieutenant had been wounded at Acre and fought on as though it hadn't weakened him. But French grenadiers had caught him and bayoneted him to death during the last night of the siege. Gamble had been unable to help him and now he clasped his sword's hilt in anguish over the death that seeped from his memory like a putrid wound. Bob should never have died there. Willoughby and Crouch should have. Life was bitterly unfair.

57

'Our men are murderers, rapists, thieves and knaves-alike. Most have had a career change on the orders of a magistrate. Crouch is no different, sir. But he's also not himself of late,' Kennedy continued. 'The men have noticed that he's started to laugh like a lunatic. He talks a lot to himself.'

'I haven't noticed,' Gamble replied carelessly.

Kennedy said nothing of his captain's ignorance. 'He's a changed man. Willoughby says ever since Acre he's been having nightmares. He dreams of blood and smoke and bodies.'

Gamble grunted, understanding the man's secret agony of having to deal with the aftermath of battle. The smell of death, powder smoke and roasting bodies came to him like a living nightmare. He breathed in Gozo's air, which was as fresh as a sunlit summer meadow by comparison. Should he show empathy? Would that be a sign of weakness? What would the company think of him? Battle-scarred and battle-weary? Here comes Captain Gamble, a man affected by war. Would they smile and laugh at him? He rubbed his face, deciding that he needed to bury those thoughts, and that he needed sleep even more.

'What are you saying? That he should be forgiven?'

'No, sir. Just understood.'

Gamble gave his friend a sharp meaningful glance. 'Harry ‾ '

Kennedy held up a hand to placate the interruption. 'I'm not trying to be impudent. I know my place. Crouch has been in his cups ever since that dreadful siege. I think he's been affected by it.'

Haven't we all? Gamble said inwardly. His fingers found his mother's silk handkerchief and twisted the cloth as images of the siege played over in his mind. Carstairs had mocked the chaplain's prayers on the eve of the fight. *"But if there is harm, then you shall pay life for life"*. They had laughed like idiots, but somehow he could not get the axiom from his mind.

'What do you intend to do, sir?' Kennedy sounded contrite.

Gamble was jarred back to reality. 'I honestly don't know. Keep him under a close watch. I'll have to consider the punishment once the mission is complete.'

'Thank you,' Kennedy said, clearly pleased. He was a clever man and liked to feel that anything could be understood, and any problem solved.

'But if he steps out of line ‾ '

'He won't,' Kennedy interjected. 'I'll make sure he doesn't.'

'Perhaps a French musket ball might find him first,' Gamble said, earning a somewhat chastising grunt from his lieutenant.

The cart had long been examined, and disappointedly contained nothing of value; old crates, sacks and fish and eel traps destined to take back to the fort full of provisions. The prisoners of war dug graves with captured spades for their fallen and the marines dug for their dead.

By dusk the sun had paled to a shimmering gold disc, hovering on the horizon like a stone flung across the sea. The water twinkled with a molten light.

Zeppi had left to meet Grech and the rest of the volunteers and so the marines waited for them where they had destroyed the French convoy. Gamble had allowed the men to rest and now a half-dozen fires lit the coast where the redcoats ate, drank, smoked and where the prisoners sat in sullen silence.

'Sir,' a voice called.

Gamble looked up from the flames where he and Kennedy shared a skin of wine, the order being that his men were allowed to drink for the day's success, but not enough to get them drunk.

'What is it, Sam?'

The lieutenant limped past a cluster of rocks. 'The French captain, sir, he asked me to come and see you.'

'And?'

'He wants to know if you have punished Marine Crouch.'

'What?' Kennedy laughed derisively.

Gamble considered his reply whilst sucking the wineskin. 'What's the bugger's name?'

'*Capitaine* Tessier, sir.'

'You tell Tessier I said I would deal with Crouch,' he said with a stern expression, 'and anything more is none of his concern.'

'Yes, sir.' Riding-Smyth turned to walk away.

'And explain that I've allowed him as an officer to keep his sword sheathed. Tell him I'd appreciate if he could do that with his goddamn mouth too. If the bugger can't, then I'm more than happy to.'

Riding-Smyth hesitated, then smiled. 'I will, sir.'

'The cheeky bastard,' Kennedy said, when Riding-Smyth had walked away, wincing from his blistered feet.

'Most of the Frogs are,' Gamble said boorishly, glaring at his timepiece. He snapped the lid shut and got up to stretch his long legs. 'Zeppi better be back here soon. I gave him strict instructions to be back here by six of the clock.'

'He will,' Kennedy replied, checking his own timepiece. It showed ten minutes after.

'I'm going to check on the picquets.'

'Would you like me to do that?'

'No, it's all right. I fancy a walk.'

Gamble picked his way through the tumble of rocks to check on the prisoners first. Dark faces glowered malevolently back, but Gamble ignored them. Riding-Smyth and the French officer were deep in conversation further down so he ignored them too. Powell and ten marines stood on guard and Gamble shared a cup of hot tea and a joke with them before climbing up to the rocks where Coppinger watched the roads. A hundred yards away to the west, atop flat rocks where the dead French horseman had been dragged by his mount, Marsh gave him a nod.

'Things quiet, Coppinger?' he asked, thrusting a steaming mug of tea into his hands. The Dane gratefully accepted it, because the sea-wind was biting.

'Yes, sir. Quiet as a pauper's funeral.'

Gamble watched bats flit from the rocks, twirling and dancing as they hunted insects, until returning to their roost nearby.

'We'll be making our way to the fort soon enough.'

'That's good, sir. I can't abide the wait any longer.' The Dane took a long drink. 'What will happen to the prisoners?'

'I had thought about sending them back to the Prince of Waves, but on second thoughts, I'll turn them over to the Gozitans until the island is in our hands,' Gamble said. 'They can throw the bloody lot of them in one of the keeps.'

'And let them rot, sir?'

Gamble chuckled. 'Perhaps. Once we've won, they'll be quickly repatriated.'

Coppinger sniffed to signify that he did not understand.

'Sent home,' Gamble answered.

They listened to the sounds of the sea, the murmur of voices and the wind that caressed the land around them.

'Can I ask you something, sir?'

'Yes.'

'It's personal, sir.'

'Go on.'

The Dane took another long swig. 'Have you ever loved a woman?'

Gamble winced and shifted his feet in awkwardness at the question. 'I've had the odd infatuation, Coppinger. I don't know if I've loved them, though. I've bedded a lot of them, but can you ever love a whore?'

'I loved a girl once.'

'A whore?'

'No, sir,' Coppinger said reprovingly.

'Oh.'

'I've been thinking a lot about her lately.'

'True love, was it?'

The marine grinned. 'I was smitten with her. Drunk with her.'

'What happened?'

'She loved another and moved away when he died.'

Gamble stared at him.

The Dane drew the cup to his lips, eyes blinking with dark secrets.

Gamble searched for better, less conventional words, but could not find them. 'How unfortunate,' he answered.

There was a commotion of sorts below and he suspected it was Powell finding a marine drunk, or that two of his men had come to blows. There was a sudden cry and he leapt down the rocks, knowing it was more than just a scuffle.

'What the hell's going on?' he shouted as a musket fired down by the shore. Marines were sprinting past and another firearm pounded the air.

'The Frenchie officer, sir,' Corporal Forge said. His bayonet-tipped musket, and those of six other men, held back the prisoners who were wide-eyed and frantic. 'He's done a runner.'

'What?' Gamble was incredulous.

'Down here, sir! The bastard's broken his parole!' Sergeant Powell waved a hand urgently and Gamble ran towards him. There was a marine in the centre of a bowl-shaped hollow, clutching his belly. It was Riding-Smyth. 'I told him to stay back.'

'Jesus,' Gamble said at the blood.

'The Froggie was angry. I told the lieutenant to stay back, sir,' Powell sounded as astonished as he was angry. 'The lieutenant tried to stop the Froggie from running, but he ran him through with his sword. I couldn't stop him, sir. I couldn't stop him. I'm sorry.'

Gamble twisted his neck up at the rocks. 'Pace! Pace!' he called desperately. 'Harry!'

'I told him ‾ ' Powell began.

'I told him to stay back, I know! Now shut up, Archie!'

'Here, sir!' Kennedy panted.

'Sir...' Riding-Smyth said, but was unable to finish. His face was pale, his lips going blue.

'Don't talk, Sam,' Gamble said, watching the blood pool between the lieutenant's fingers. Riding-Smyth's eyes were staring up at the sky where a smattering of stars were glimmered. 'Save your breath, there's a good fellow.'

'He was livid,' Riding-Smyth said and coughed, 'and upset about the deaths.' He winced and could not help crying out in pain. 'I saw him unsheathe his sword, but I didn't do anything. I froze.'

'It's not your fault,' Gamble said, glancing up again. 'Pace! Get your arse here now!' He clasped Riding-Smyth's hand, feeling the hot sticky blood and the lieutenant's tight grasp.

'I'm here, sir!' Pace pushed his way through the gathering crowd. He dropped to the floor and tried to inspect the wound, but the lieutenant was clenching his hands over it. 'I need to see it, sir,' Pace pleaded and Riding-Smyth eased briefly. 'I need a light!' A marine quickly returned with a lantern, illuminating the gruesome wound. A heartbeat later, Pace shot his captain a grave look.

'Help him.'

Pace was solemn. 'There's nothing more I can do, sir. I'm sorry.'

Gamble, mouth twitching, reached out and grabbed Pace by the throat. 'You can save him!' he snarled.

'I can't, sir,' Pace replied.

Kennedy bent down to Gamble's height. 'Let Pace go, sir,' he said soothingly. 'Sam doesn't need to see this. There's nothing anyone can do now.'

Gamble searched Pace's eyes for hope, saw none and released his grip. His gaze turned to Riding-Smyth, who was trembling. Gamble unbuttoned his coat and draped it over his friend.

'Oh God, have mercy,' the young lieutenant said, his voice a whispering moan. 'Tell my family I did my duty.'

A prick of tears stung Gamble's eyes. Carstairs had said the same thing. 'You did your duty, Sam. I'm proud of you in the short time we've known each other.'

Riding-Smyth smiled. 'Friends, sir?'

'For life,' he assured him with a smile.

'The fort…I wanted to be there when you took it.'

'I'll take it for you and I'll kill Tessier.'

Riding-Smyth shook his head. 'He was angry. Don't take revenge.' His eyes widened, dark blood trickled from his slack mouth. 'My family . . .' He coughed up more blood.

'I'll tell them you're a hero,' Gamble cuffed away tears, unafraid who saw him. 'Ain't that right, lads? Our lieutenant of marines here is a goddamn hero.'

A chorus of hoarse agreement rose up from the men.

He gripped Riding-Smyth's hands and felt rosary beads. Pace had placed them there and Gamble thought it an act of wonderful consideration. The marine began to sing Heart of Oak, a popular song, and one Sam liked.

'I don't want to die,' Riding-Smyth said, tears flowed to mix with the blood, as Pace's voice echoed around the hollow.

I don't want you too, either, Sam, Gamble's voice collapsed with grief in his head.

Riding-Smyth closed his eyes, convulsed and a gurgling sound rattled in his throat as Gamble held him. And then, he was gone.

A moment passed where the only sound was the sea.

'Lord our God,' Kennedy said in a loud, crisp voice. 'You are always faithful and quick to show mercy. Young Samuel was violently taken from his brothers-at-sea. Come swiftly to his aid, have mercy on him, and comfort his family and friends by the power and protection of the Cross. We ask this through Christ our Lord. Amen.'

'Amen,' voices spoke in unison.

Gamble peered at Riding-Smyth's absurdly young face. Another death, and another promising friendship gone to oblivion. His hands balled into fists, blood boiling with rage – a fiery killing rage, before he managed to subdue it. He stood, blinking and stricken.

'Where did the bastard go?'

Kennedy's eyes were red-rimmed. 'He climbed down to the rocks and it was there we lost him. I presumed he jumped into the sea, but I could not tell. It is suicide to try to swim those waves. The current would take him out and he'd either drown, or be dashed upon the rocks.'

'The bastard is still alive until I see his corpse. Archie, take a dozen men and scour the coastline to the south. Harry, take a handful and search the north, just in case he tries to backtrack. The craven turd has broken his parole. He's a man with no honour and anyone who finds him will earn himself the contents of my purse! Find him and bring him to me alive,' Gamble said, the word 'alive' the ballast of the order. 'Careful, he's armed. Now go! Go!'

'What about you, sir?' Kennedy enquired, wondering what his captain would do to the prisoner.

Gamble looked down at Riding-Smyth. 'I'll stay here with him a while longer.'

*

He had not wanted to kill the young officer, but there was nothing else he could have done. Gamble had not listened and so there was only one other option. And now the redcoats were scouring every nook and cranny to find him. They looked impressive; grim and battle-hardened warriors, but though they might have a keen sense of doggedness, Tessier knew that it didn't make such men intelligent.

He had watched them scan the waves as they crashed and sucked at the tiny cove from his place of hiding. A tall redcoat stood watching the sea for movement, then jumped down to the next rock and repeated his patient observations. Another enemy jabbed at dark places, maybe just wide enough to conceal a man, with his bayonet. But an officer searching large rock pools called them on.

Tessier was about to move when he heard the tiniest footfalls behind him. He froze. Unable to fetch his horse, he had run as fast as his pumping legs could take him. Muskets fired and the lead balls whipped past him, but he had clambered down rocks, scraping the skin of his hands and knees as he descended to where the sea lapped the shore. There was a stench of something dead. Fetid. It was so powerful that it made him gag. It was coming from where a tangle of animal legs and seaweed protruded in amongst a cluster of rocks. It was a goat, its body bloated with rot, its face half-skeletal. Flies buzzed over the eye-less sockets and in and around its drooping mouth. It must have fallen into the sea, or been injured and drowned.

Tessier scanned the area wildly. There were places to hide, but they were exposed and easy to find by the enemy if they did a proper sweep. Wind brought sand into his face. A voice called. He dropped low. He couldn't see them, but the redcoats weren't far off. He had to hide and there was only one place to go.

Holding his breath, he heaved the putrid corpse carefully aside. The air was rank, sticky and choking. Flies and maggots crawled everywhere. Tessier had pulled the dead beast and stinking seaweed over him, squirming, cursing and burrowing into the foulness. There was an old expression his father used to say to him, *'you made your bed, now lie in it'*. Tessier grunted at the irony.

There wasn't much space to breathe, but there was no time to change that now. Time seemed to go slow. He couldn't hear anything, except for the buzzing of flies, rank liquid dripping and the wind buffeting the seaweed. No one came and he suspected the corpse was cutting off the sound of the enemy searching and had gone past long ago. Revulsion was forcing his fingers to move the corpse. The moisture clawed at his nose and throat, sand was filling his nostrils and he became frantic to breathe. The goat pressed harder and he wanted desperately to push his way clear, but then the first enemy appeared. Stalking as a hunter.

And now the redcoat was standing next to him. Tessier closed his eyes, unable to breathe in the noxious fumes and expecting an enemy bayonet to pierce his flesh. There was a tapping sound, and hot water trickled down his arm. The redcoat was urinating. Perhaps he was safe after all. No voices called out. No mocking laughter. After a moment, the last of the enemy moved away and Tessier tried to keep the exhilaration from bursting out of his body. He lived! He slowly pushed up and crawled free, uniform soaked with rot. He glanced around. The redcoats were going and he scrambled down to the sea, wiping jellied gore from his face. He laughed. Cool salty air was upon him and he lay on the surf, letting the water wash his body as he drew in huge gasps of breath.

He told himself he was free, but a voice in his head said that only when he had reached the fort was that true.

And when the captain of marines came, Tessier would kill him for permitting the butchery of his men.

Tessier went south.

*

The marines returned three hours later withdrawn and unable to meet their captain's gaze. They had not found Tessier. Gamble turned to stare out at the sea. He only turned back when he heard the sentries call out a warning. Behind him the road coming from Rabat was alive with armed men. Zeppi had brought the volunteers. There must have been a hundred of them.

'Baldassar will bring the others from the north and the west,' Zeppi smiled proudly. 'They will come and we will take back our island.' He noticed a cold emptiness in the camp. Gamble stood over a freshly dug mound, his breeches and shirt filthy with dirt and sweat. Kennedy explained and Zeppi stood appalled.

'Sam was a catholic,' Gamble uttered to his friend, 'so I want a proper prayer said for him. Can you do that for me?'

Zeppi swallowed hard. 'Of course,' he said, gripping Gamble's forearm. He stood over the grave and said a prayer in Maltese.

'I'm going to get him for what he did,' Gamble said when Zeppi had finished, not caring who heard him. Marsh had brought him a bucket of seawater in the meantime to wash himself of the filth.

'It wasn't your fault, sir,' Kennedy said.

Gamble growled as he washed. It felt as though he was manacled with heavy chains around his heart. With every move they tightened like a noose. 'I'll murder him. I'll goddamn slaughter the beak-nosed bastard.'

'You weren't to know he would break his parole.'

Gamble rounded on him, eyes full of accusation. 'And perhaps if I had strung Crouch up in the first place, then maybe Sam would still be alive?'

Kennedy looked full of remorse, knowing he had championed the marine's innocence. 'It doesn't matter what you did, or didn't do, sir,' he said, trying to mollify the situation. 'Sam did say not to seek revenge.'

'You think I'm going to let Tessier get away with the murder of one of my officers?' Gamble snarled as he pulled on his coat.

Kennedy knew better than to question his friend's resolve. 'No, sir.'

'Then why did you damn well say it?'

'I think Sam was trying to keep you from the torment of retribution . . .' Kennedy left the thought unfinished.

Gamble blinked bloodshot eyes. 'It's too late for that,' his voice sank to a whisper, as though he didn't want Kennedy to hear the words.

'He should not have murdered our friend,' Kennedy said. 'The blame is with him, not with you or me. Even the prisoners seem shocked by it.'

Gamble's jaw clenched in anger. 'Christ, Harry, but it was my decision to let him keep his sword!'

'It was a matter of honour.'

Gamble spat. 'Damn his honour! He preached that damned word to me! I'll show him how honourable I can be! Sergeant Powell! Form the men up!'

'Sir!'

'And Archie?'

'Sir?'

'Give the Frog's horse to the locals,' Gamble said. 'It'll give them something to eat.'

The Gozitans went first, taking the tracks across the hills to the south, ever conscious of the fort's watchful gaze over the last ridgeline. The marines followed them; the wounded lay in the oxen-pulled cart. Gamble was the last to leave. His eyes raked over the road to where a brave feat was soured by the needless death of his lieutenant. He had blistered his hands digging, but at least the grave had a cross, and his lieutenant's name carved into it and now a respectable prayer said for him. Other fallen soldiers had not been so lucky.

Gamble forced the march hard. The wind picked up a little which swirled dust into mouths and eyes. Feet became sore, muscles burned and soon, he heard the inexorable sounds of grousing from the ranks.

'If I hear any more whining from anyone, I'll beat the man to death with my bare hands!' Gamble snapped for no other reason than that he felt like shouting.

The mixed force reached the cove and lit a fire at the shoreline. He noticed that a handful of the Gozitans were leaning on their weapons, panting for breath. One man collapsed onto the sand. For a moment, Gamble wanted to savage them for their weakness, but he knew that was wrong and that they weren't even soldiers. He took a deep breath to dispel his irritation.

The *Sea Prince* saw the beacon, and by midnight, as a soft rain fell, two longboats were dragged up the sandy beach. The smell of stale breath, sweat and damp wool washed over him.

A group of officers formed the sailors up. Gamble had expected to see the landing party commanded by the charismatic Captain James Eaton or First Lieutenant John Greenslade, naval officers of senior rank, and both men always liked to be in the thick of action. He was pleasantly surprised to see Benjamin Pym at their head. Pym was a naval lieutenant, a rank equivalent to Gamble's rank as a land captain.

'Not here to step on your toes, Simon,' Pym said in his thick Cornish accent, stretching out his hand in friendship, which Gamble took warmly. Pym wore his plain blue naval uniform over white breeches and stockings. A pistol was tucked in his sword belt, and a curved sword taken from a Turk at Acre hung at his left hip. 'The command of this here landing party was the subject of a good wager on a ferocious game of cards.' Pym was accompanied by Brownrigg the Boatswain, Rooke the Boatswain's Mate and two junior Midshipmen keen to make a reputation for themselves.

'And you won?'

'No, I lost the bloody game,' Pym grinned, his hazel eyes glinting in his freckled face.

'Lieutenant Pym wanted to bring your damned leg-humping dog along,' Brownrigg scowled. 'I ain't having that mutt with me so it stayed behind.'

'It's a shame because it's certainly got sweeter breath than you,' Pym said with a shrug.

Everyone laughed.

'You got any advice for these young idiots with salt for brains?' Brownrigg gestured at the Midshipmen who blushed under scrutiny.

Gamble frowned. 'Just don't get killed,' he said, causing a wave of laughter. He turned to Pym. 'It's good to see you here, Ben,' he said with genuine affection. He considered both Pym and Kennedy as able and dependable friends.

'So what's happened? The mission going well for you bootnecks?' Pym grinned at the moniker the Jack Tars gave the marines, which they considered the leather stock as bits cut from boots. He craned to look over Gamble's broad shoulders to see Kennedy's crestfallen expression. There was no Riding-Smyth and Pym's gaze flicked back to Gamble who suddenly looked crushed. 'Sweet Christ,' he said, dipping his head in respect.

'A French officer, who I allowed to keep his blade, killed him with it before fleeing,' Gamble announced evenly, and was inwardly surprised by his calmness.

'Broke his parole, did he? The cowardly, contemptible devil!'

'Aye.'

'Where's he gone? To the fort?'

'Yes, and I assume the Crapauds now know we're here.'

Pym sighed with bitter understanding, because he assumed the mission was over and the men would have to go back on board. 'So now what?' He glared at the Gozitans and grimaced. 'Not exactly armed to the teeth, are they? Are they willing to fight?'

Gamble turned to them. 'They certainly are. My guide tells me when their blood is up, nothing on earth will stop them. This is their land and they understandably want it back.'

'Good for them,' Pym grinned cheerfully, then looked around.

Gamble caught him looking almost disdainfully at his uniform. He knew that naval officers were jealous that their land counterparts wore lace, gorgets, epaulettes and sashes. As Naval officers, they were not permitted to, and constantly grumbled about the dullness of their plain frock coats.

'You might even take a lovely Frog officer's coat with gold lace,' Gamble teased, 'if that would make you feel any better?'

Pym gave a lop-sided grin. 'Anything that would dazzle more than the scarlet rag of a ragamuffin you wear.' He gave Gamble's elbow and forearm a theatrical inspection. 'Where's the material gone? Have you lost it? There's more shirt on show than coat.' He let the mirth settle, then looked serious. 'Then we continue?'

Excited chatter came from the seamen until Rooke threatened them with his starter, a length of rope used for enforcing discipline on the ships' decks. They were dressed in round hats, their slops were blue jackets, light or striped trousers, stockings and buckled shoes. They carried muskets, pikes, swords and pistols. They certainly did not want to go back to the ship - and neither did Gamble.

'We still go ahead with the plan,' Gamble said. 'Vengeance is - '

'Golden,' Pym cut in. 'Like sunshine after rain. The lads are keen for a spot of killing. Aye, we're all here for that. Cooped up too long and my ears have heard some of the coarsest language known to man. I've told them the Toads are guarding strongboxes of gold and that there is a harem of buxom whores in the fort in need of rescuing,' he grinned. He cocked his head up to the hills where thin

72

veils of rain drifted towards them. 'Maybe I'm wrong and perhaps there will be treasures inside? I could do with recouping last night's losses at cards.' He looked wistful. 'But in truth they don't need to be coaxed. They'll do as they're told. We'll take the damned fort and you can murder that French bastard.'

'Before I disembarked, I asked you to bring something.'

'I have it,' Pym patted a bundle underneath his coat.

Gamble nodded grimly. He stepped away momentarily to gaze up at the sky where until the moon rose, there had been only pale starlight.

Pym lit a cigar. 'I pity the man who did what he did to Sam,' he said to Kennedy, out of ear-shot. 'He's about to wish he hadn't been born.'

Kennedy peered at Gamble's back. 'He's got a heart of oak, sir. I don't know of any other man as tough.'

'He's hard all right,' Pym said. 'Like Cornish granite.'

'I know the captain's hurting. Losing Bob hurt him deep, but now losing Sam . . .' Kennedy's voice trailed away.

'That French bastard is a dead man.'

'Aye, sir.'

Gamble turned around, face impassive. 'Ready?' he asked Pym.

'As I'll ever be.'

'Then let's go.'

Gamble would take his cutlass to the enemy behind their walls and, in the oncoming fray, would slaughter Tessier.

*

Général Évrard Chasse, commanding officer of Fort Dominance, could not bear the reek anymore.

He left his desk where maps and parchments had transformed the plain stone room into a map room of sorts. A tapestry showing the construction of the fort by the Grand Master, hung along one wall. An ancient sword, all rust, hung from the other and it suited the general. Chasse was a proud, fussy man who harboured a suspicion that the French command did not appreciate his military brilliance. He had fought the Prussians at Valmy, the Austrians at Jemappes and Rivoli, and yet, he commanded the fort on a remote island far from home. Bonaparte had secured his involvement in the campaign and now he felt slighted. He had once been given the command of a division, but now a garrison of three hundred men. A third of them were conscripts and seamen with no fighting experience, another was mostly veterans and the others were sick; languishing in the hospital beds, or confined to their quarters. The damn islands were fever-ridden.

He sighed despondently and peered out of the windows with tired-looking eyes. Far across the water he could see Malta where *Général* Claude-Henri Belgrand de Vaubois commanded Valletta. Chasse gave the island a sneer. Damn Vaubois! Loved by Bonaparte, all because he had once been an artillery officer! When his commission as *Commandant en chef des Isles de Malte et du Goze* was announced, the toadying junior officers had crowded around him like flies on a turd. The old saying proved it: *"It's not what you know, it's who you know"*.

The peasants had risen up and now Chasse found that he was not a commander, or a governor of Gozo, but a prisoner. A damned hostage trapped in a bolthole, on a flea-bitten and diseased island that nobody in their right mind would want. He had once thought these islands were ripe for the plucking, but no more. He hated being here.

'Sir?'

Chasse sighed again and rubbed the whiskers on his chin.

'Sir?' This time the voice was more urgent.

Chasse looked back at the man with the raw-boned face standing at the door. He glowered with fierce eyes like an unruly hound.

'So who was this man?' he asked Tessier, with distaste because he could still smell the rankness coming from him from the far side of the room. The incense burning in a pot did nothing to alleviate the smell.

'*Capitaine* Gamble. An Englishman, sir.'

'What regiment were these *les rosbifs* allegedly from?'

Tessier's hands contracted in anger at the thought of the punishing volley fire. He had thought the English were supposed to be raw soldiers and badly led, but the marines were anything but. He straightened stiffly as he responded. 'They're not alleged, sir. They are marines. They have taken the northern redoubt and ambushed my men who were out collecting provisions.'

Chasse gave a small mocking laugh. 'How do you know it has been taken? Are you sure it's not just a local force? It's not the first time we've seen an armed insurrection.'

Tessier blew out a lungful of air. 'No, *Général*. They are English. Redcoats. I presumed they would have seized it before marching south for they would not want an enemy garrison at their rear. I would have done so. They captured me and I escaped.'

Chasse waved a hand as though he was finding the report a nuisance. 'Yes, yes, you already told me that. You managed to cut your bonds and flee.'

Tessier said nothing at the lie.

'What of your men?' Chasse asked.

'Alas, I could not free them, sir. It was a terrible decision to leave, but I had little choice.'

The *général* grunted and continued stroking his beard and moustache. 'Then you hid underneath a rotting sheep and escaped.'

'I said it was a goat,' Tessier corrected, forgetting his manners. He couldn't help but stare at Chasse's facial hair that looked like a vagina's fringe. It was thick and curly and the *général* had no idea of a cruel and offensive nickname that was bestowed on him by the garrison: *'la chatte'*.

Chasse twitched. 'Goat! Sheep! Whatever! What are English marines doing here, *Capitaine*? Why land here when Valletta is blockaded by their ships? How many marines was it? Fifty?' The *général* laughed unpleasantly and stepped forward to pour himself some wine, then remembered the smell so pretended to stretch instead. Fingers drummed the wall.

'They murdered two of my men in cold blood.' Tessier's jaw clenched. 'They were surrendering and a damned redcoat butchered them.'

'Awful things happen in war,' Chasse spat.

'They pounced like a pack of hungry wolves. They killed Prost, Raffin and Fievet,' he said of the dead officers. 'This Gamble has no honour like his animals,' Tessier was beginning to feel that the *général* wasn't taking his accusation seriously enough. 'He is a devil!'

Chasse watched him before speaking, and rubbed the soft bulges of skin under his eyes. He had already marked Tessier down as an impetuous man. 'I think you are a sore loser, *Capitaine*. I think you are still smarting from the ambush and the anger is clouding your judgement. Snap out of it! I asked you, why would the English land just fifty men here?'

Tessier paused, then frowned. 'I don't know, sir.'

'No, you clearly do not,' Chasse waved a finger at him, ignoring the details to concentrate on something far more important. 'The English would never send just fifty men. Are they here to take this fort? A company of them?' He laughed mirthlessly.

'Sir, more of them must have landed ⁻ '

Chasse slapped the wall with a hand, then glared with protruding eyes at the dishevelled officer who was clouding his favourite room with his foul odour. 'You're an idiot, *Capitaine*! There is no sign of any approaching English force. The hills are bare of marching troops and the coast is clear of warships. The English must have sent a scouting party to survey the island, or perhaps it was a local rabble dressed in the uniform to trick you. That's all it is, and I won't have another word said on the matter. You're safe behind thick walls. Stop panicking. You'll make our men nervous of shadows.'

'Shadows didn't kill my men.'

'Were you distracted?'

'Sir?'

'You must have been. You walked straight into an ambush. Or were you simply docile? Too much sun, perhaps?'

'*Général*?'

'Where were your men who should have been walking ahead of the convoy in order to expel such an attack?'

'It was not quite like that ˉ '

'Yes, it was!' Chasse interrupted by slapping the wall again. 'You were careless. Your men were careless.' A lot of the men from the early revolutionary days had become ill-disciplined, or had become riddled with bad habits after the easy victories in Italy and Chasse considered Tessier was one of those men. 'You led your men into the trap,' he continued. 'It was nobody else's fault. If you want someone to blame, then look no further than yourself.'

Tessier's eyes narrowed. 'The English devils will come here, *Général*. Remember it was I who told you this.'

'They will not come here! They will go to Valletta! And you, *Capitaine* will go and take a bath! Take two and take a whetstone to your wits! They need sharpening! Now vacate this room before you bring in more flies! Go! Leave me!'

Tessier, an incandescent anger about to burst from every vein, slammed a hand into the wall outside the *général's* room. The damned *les rosbifs* were here and he knew they would march on the fort soon.

Then, let the marines come here, he said to himself. *Let them die against the walls of Dominance.*

*

It was Sunday and six monks climbed the road cut through the hill called Ras it-Tafal when the dawn light was nothing more than an orange glow above the western horizon. The sunken road straightened and then the huge limestone walls of Fort Dominance rose up from the rocky landscape, obliterating everything else. Weeds and wind-blown grasses, dark in the morning light, hugged the stonework. The French Tricolour flew high from the imposing battlements, but the Gozitan monks were allowed to say mass in the chapel dedicated to the Blessed Virgin Mary of Graces every Sabbath day.

Sentries watched the priests approach as they crossed the stone bridge over a wide ditch to the fort's main gate, a path designed for just one wagon to cross at once. The gates were of the Baroque style with an inscription in Latin above the archway commemorating the fort's completion. One of the monks, tall and straight-backed, carried a simple wooden cross, whilst two carried a long oblong box, decorated with gold crosses. They stopped underneath the gate's archway where a portcullis blocked their entrance. Dust, kicked up by their feet, wafted in the air. Beyond the curtain wall to their left, and towering above a gun emplacement that guarded the woodland to the east, was the Notre Dame Bastion. To the right was a huge counterguard where figures scoured the hills for enemies from behind thick embrasures.

A French guard, grey-haired and puffing on a lit pipe, walked over to the gate. Two other guards, watching the monks, their eyes full of scrutiny, returned to their conversation with coarse laughter. The leading monk spoke hurried French and the guard mumbled to himself before disappearing back into the fort's courtyard.

'Where's the bastard gone, sir?' Sergeant Powell growled from somewhere in his shadowed habit.

'To fetch the officer of the guard,' Zeppi replied. Immediately, Gamble wondered whether this would be Tessier and the French may have imposed stricter concessions for entering the fort. After all, the French had dissolved all religious activities and it was only the governor's whim that allowed entry. 'Don't worry, I know the man,' he continued. 'He is cheerful and polite. We will be let in without further delay. Monks are always allowed.'

'Good, because this robe stinks like a sick goat, and sooner I can cast it off the better I'll be,' Powell grumbled.

The fort was silent; a stillness that frayed nerves.

'He's been gone a long time,' Powell rasped, splintering the quiet. 'It will not be easy if this bluff doesn't work?'

'Not long now, Archie,' Gamble smiled, and the sergeant saw a flash of white in the recesses of the hood. 'Remember: wait for my word and be quick.'

'We're like avenging angels, come to the French with swords to smite them down,' Zeppi's lips curled like a fed cat settling into its basket.

'And axes,' Powell muttered.

Boots thudded and a young officer greeted them. It was not Tessier. He was curious to know what was in the long box. Zeppi said something to him and the officer smiled and stepped back. He shouted up to the gatehouse and a voice replied.

'I told him we carried the sacred bones of St Giuseppe of Nadur, and this is a portable shrine,' Zeppi whispered.

'Not heard of that saint before,' Powell said.

'I made it up, Sergeant,' Zeppi said with a smirk.

'Do you think he believed you?'

'Perhaps,' Zeppi replied. 'Depends how suspicious he is. Or how gullible.'

'It's going to work,' Gamble said confidently.

'If I were them, I'd have killed us all by now,' Powell said. 'Why didn't they send out a demi-brigade to see us off?'

'Perhaps Sam's killer didn't come back here.' Zeppi mused. 'Maybe he fled elsewhere?'

'He came here,' Gamble said. 'It's the only safe place for him on the island.'

'So why haven't I seen any Frenchies come after us?' Powell said, scratching his crotch.

Gamble glanced up at the main gate, fingers clenching in the delay. 'He probably feels safe behind these walls and knows we'll be coming for him anyway. Why make it easy?'

'Or maybe he told no one?' Zeppi hazarded a guess.

Gamble shook his head. 'Why would he keep our presence a secret?'

'They don't appear to be on alert, sir,' Powell said.

'Agreed,' Gamble replied. 'And that's good news for us. We should take heart for this isn't a trap.'

The sound of gears turning and chains jangling rent the air and Gamble wondered if the barracks would be alarmed by the din, but then considered this was normal practice and he was allowing nerves to give his confidence a full broadside. Fear was giving the attack a desperate impetus.

The portcullis juddered to a halt and the officer waved them forward. The pipe-smoking guard smiled pleasantly and stepped out under the great iron teeth to the stone bridge to see what the new day would bring.

'Now,' Gamble said.

Zeppi went first and Gamble followed. At the moment of passing the officer, Gamble stooped and the Frenchman thought the monk had stumbled. He reached down to help him up and never saw the dirk that plunged into his heart. Gamble twisted it free and left the enemy bleeding and twitching on the ground. Adams slunk up the steps to the gatehouse and Gamble heard a soft sigh and then returned giving a curt nod of success. Good, the gatehouse was theirs. Coppinger walked up to the grey-haired guard and cut his throat from behind. The body toppled over the stone walkway and fell with a thud into the ditch below.

Powell pulled free his axes, letting their short haft fall through his hands until he was satisfied he had better grip. He calmly walked over to the two guards to the left of the gatehouse. He glanced up at the huge ravine, shaped like an enormous ships prow, saw no one looking down from the slanted openings and thumped his right axe into the nearest Frenchman's back. The man collapsed, and Powell yanked it free with a horrid sucking sound. The other Frenchman stood gaping at the axe-wielding monk and then understood this was no priest at all. He tried to bring up his musket when Powell knocked it aside with his left axe and then chopped his other axe into the foe's breastbone. The force knocked the guard onto the dusty ground, letting out a horrid, pathetic sigh. Blood spurted from his chest and bubbled at his mouth as he groaned. Powell mercifully and swiftly chopped down through his throat, the second blow severing his spinal cord.

'Get the weapon's out,' Gamble ordered and Marsh opened the box to reveal muskets and swords. They threw off their disguises and buckled swords, slid bayonets from their scabbards, slipped the rings over muzzles and slotted them into place. There was something reassuringly determined at the sound of fixed bayonets. Powell pulled the dying men out of sight, tucked the axes in his belt and Gamble threw him his musketoon. They then cocked their firearms.

All was quiet.

No one had seen them, no one had raised the alarm; but there were still two more gates to access. Trusting his instincts Gamble suspected the first would be open, but the second would be locked. It would be impossible to open, but Gamble had already thought of that. Deep in the shadows, he craned his neck up at the ravine. The opening was across a wide dry moat, and from here Gamble knew they would have to scramble through the ravine to likely cross another bridge to get to the main gate.

It was time for Kennedy and Pym to come. 'Now!' he called out and Coppinger waved from the outer gate to the road.

It was five o'clock.

*

'Not long now, lads,' Kennedy's voice called softly. 'We wait for the signal and then we'll rush the bastards!'

'That's right, boys,' Pym said, 'plunder and whores await your eager fingers! Tits so big and nipples so hard you can hang your muskets on them! Stay hidden now!'

The marines and landing party were crouched down on the road, some lying flat. A marine jumped at a running lizard. Another marine laughed at him, and Corporal Forge slapped him across the head. 'Quiet now!'

Men scraped sharpening stones down their blades. The sharp, grating noise made the hairs on Kennedy's neck stand up on end. Pym felt the edge of his curved sword with his thumb. Another prayed and one of the Midshipmen vomited.

'Nearly time,' Kennedy called out, checking the timepiece in his palm. A bead of sweat landed on the watch face and he carefully wiped it away with a finger. It had been his grandfather's and he would take it back home one day.

It would be good, he pondered, to go home and see the new century for it was only a few months away. Perhaps the eighteen hundreds would bring him a wife, wealth and a captaincy. Maybe the world would change for the better and all the wars would end. But he suspected, the politicians would always need men trained to kill; it was the way of the world. Peace would not last long.

Kennedy saw movement and his heart raced. Gamble had secured the outer gate.

'There's the signal, boys! Up! Up! Let's go!'

*

The six men ran to the ravine, a distance of thirty feet. Gamble expected an enemy to call out, but it was eerily silent. He slammed against the ravine's gap and peered around the wall. The entrance led to a set of winding stairs. Gamble, took the steps carefully, sword in hand. Shadowed light flashed bright and he edged to the entryway. Directly to their right lay the walkway to the main gate. Gamble could not see any enemies there. Up above on the firing steps were two Frenchmen. The first was playing cards on a block of stone next to a glowing brazier. The smoke wafted pungent scents down towards the marines. The second was staring across the outer walls to where, above the wooded slopes that edged to the sea, birds flew from the tree tops. Something had startled them and Gamble knew what that was. His eyes flicked up at the fort's curtain walls, seeing movement along the parapet but no faces peered curiously down. The card-playing one was the nearest and caught sight of Gamble out of the corner of his eye. Before he could react, Gamble prodded man's Adam's apple with his cutlass. The Frenchman gulped loudly and his colleague turned to the sound. He reacted more quickly and brought his musket to bear. Gamble hammered it aside as the weapon fired, its discharge echoing like a death knell. The ball ricocheted off the wall. Gamble knew their infiltration was over, but they still had the advantage for now.

The seated Frenchman stood to pull free his *sabre-briquet*, but Gamble swung his sword back across his body to cleave through the man's neck. The enemy slumped over the stone, twitching as the blood fountained over the fallen cards. The other man charged Gamble, hefting the unloaded musket to batter him down. Gamble dodged to one side, kicked at the Frenchman and lunged. The blade went under the guard's arm, up through his armpit and into his chest cavity. He gasped, fell and Gamble turned with his reddened sword, seeing a shape appear at the stairs.

It was Powell. 'The Toads know we're here, sir!' he said urgently.

'I damn well know!' Gamble snapped.

'*Qui vive?*' a voice called out. The challenge was repeated.

'Ignore them,' Gamble said.

Other French voices called down from the parapets and Gamble saw movement on the inner wall. The enemy was running down to a flank battery. Three cannons, their muzzles pointing at the trees beyond the ramparts, were stirred to life by the gunners. He knew why, but they did not concern him.

The French gathering at the main gate did.

'*Merde! Les Anglais!*'

*

'Fire!' Baldassar Grech shouted. Muskets blasted up from the trees, the shots pocked the thick walls and caused no injuries, but that was not the intention. 'Keep firing! Let our enemies know we're here! For God and Gozo!'

84

The Gozitans cheered and fired and reloaded as dirty white smoke fogged the woodland. Each man wore a cloth badge pinned to their chest showing a white Maltese cross on a black field. A Gozitan saw an enemy figure high up at the Notre Dame Bastion, and aimed his musket and pulled the trigger. He peered past the plume of noxious cloud to see that the enemy was still there.

'You're not going to hit him from this distance, Micallef,' Grech laughed sourly. 'Our objective is to keep the French busy whilst the British assault the fort.'

'I don't trust them!' Micallef growled back. He had grey hair, and skin the texture of leather. 'The British said they would land an army, but they haven't even managed to send a single regiment yet. Do you know what I think?'

'What?'

'I think they are bluffing. They will only land proper soldiers after we have done all the work!'

'You're forgetting about the marines,' a drover named Camilleri said reproachfully.

Micallef threw his arms up in frustration. 'The French are still here, you fool!' He stuck his thumb at the fort.

'The British supplied the muskets and pistols,' Camilleri said patiently, loading his musket with untrained slowness. 'They armed the Maltese and they took the forts.'

Micallef spat to show his indignation. 'So they give us the guns to do the work for them. That way we lose many men and they won't. Ask yourself why do they fight? For us? No. They fight for the gold of Protestant England.'

'What are you babbling about?'

'Have you ever been there?'

'No.'

Micallef crossed himself. 'It's a vile land full of people inclined to criminality.' The others were silent and given a voice, he continued.

'They will see us killed and they will steal our lands. They will rob us as the French did, and you are both fools enough not to see that.'

Grech understood the man's distrust. 'Give them a chance to prove themselves. I did not want them here either. I was ignorant and that allowed prejudice to speak instead of embracing them as allies. They have lost men for our country. Does that not speak to you of their purpose? Today is the Lord's Day and that is a good omen. Once I see red coats on the walls, we'll make our move. Until then, and with the grace of God, we keep firing and we'll have victory soon.'

*

'Open the portcullis!' *Capitaine* Tessier demanded. 'Open it!'

The redcoats had reached the ravine, but there was nowhere else they could go to. If they jumped or fell, they would find themselves in the dry-moat where they would have to find the handful of accessible places to climb out. Even if they managed this feat, they would then come face-to-face with a bone-shattering drop separating them from the outer ramparts.

A trumpet blared and the sound of musketry hammered the eastern walls. The French soldiers were piling out of the barrack block, sprinting to the gates, buttoning their jackets and loading their firearms. The enemy was here, but the fools in the gatehouse were not hauling up the portcullis.

'You imbeciles! Open them!' Tessier banged on the thick metal bars with his sword.

The redcoats had to be stopped quickly before they took hold. He saw men wearing naval dress and knew that he had been right all along. From the moment the first musket shot punctured the morning's air, he knew Gamble was here. The English had landed more men on the island. Goddamn Chasse's obstinacy! Tessier could see the officer and knew it was Gamble. Tessier would kill him and eject the impudent English from the fort. He would shame the general for his incompetence, and be promoted to colonel by noon.

But the portcullis remained down and Tessier could only watch helplessly as the redcoats swarmed the defences.

*

Gamble gazed north from the ravine to see the marines and Jack Tars sprinting over the lip of the road, bayonet-scabbards, cartridge boxes and haversacks bouncing with each stride.

Suddenly, a boom of gunfire rocked the air. Gunners stationed in the St Paul's Bastion had fired a cannon and he saw one of the sailors torn to bloody gristle by the ball's terrible strike. The projectile, spattered-red, slammed into the banks of the road, churning earth high up in the air. A second gun fired sending the ball too high and he saw the ball clip the embankment, spin, and plummet down the hill's incline.

'Come on, you bastards!' Gamble shouted at his men, as the fastest reached the first stone walkway. 'Move your arses! Move!'

The seamen were the slowest because they carried cumbersome ladders, required to scale the inner wall. Gamble knew there would be no way to get through the gate, so the marines had to climb over the walls and take the fort by escalade. Riding-Smyth had questioned the method and now he could feel fear sniping at his confidence, but if they could climb the walls, half the fight was done.

A third gun was awoken and had its throat blasted free, but the seamen were now clear of its shot, and the first redcoats had reached the ravine. A crackle of musketry fired ineffectively at them from the main gate.

'Sergeant Powell!' Gamble ordered. 'One platoon to form on the bridge, the other to grasp the ladders!'

'Sir!'

The seamen could not hope to bring the ladders up the stairway, so they were placed against the ravine's high walls and the marines hauled them up and over the parapets. The portcullis was still down and Gamble wondered if the French officers had ordered it. He could see a handful of officers there but wasn't sure if one was Tessier.

'Faster!' he bellowed, glancing at the main gate and up at the inner wall where musket muzzles flashed leaving the embrasures ringed with flame, but the bullets caused no harm. The gunners on the emplacement were busy firing muskets at Grech's men and packing the cannons with grapeshot. Then, the great guns jerked to life and the battery instantly clouded white. The air was shattered with the percussive explosions. Gamble knew he had to scale the ladder, climb down the parapet and silence those guns. For now, he had to hope that Grech was still alive and that he had to get the Gozitan-built ladders in place.

'Heave!' Rooke the Boatswain's Mate, called from the ravine as the seamen pushed two ladders up for the marines to haul.

'Come on!' Gamble pushed a faltering soldier to one side and gripped the top rung. He brought the ladder down over the parapet to where Kennedy waited. 'We can't wait any longer, Harry! Get the two ladders to the gate now! The other four will have to wait.'

'Sir!' Kennedy spun on his heels. 'Platoon! Advance!'

'Fix bayonets!' Gamble ordered, as there would be little or no time to do so later. He turned and cupped a hand to his mouth. 'Lieutenant Pym! I want your pikes! Now if you please!'

'You'll be getting them soon enough, Captain Gamble!' Pym replied as more of the landing party reached the ravine's upper level. 'Come on! Get those bloody ladders over the wall!'

Gamble jumped the steps. 'Marines! To me!' He sprinted after the advancing men. Muskets crashed from the ramparts above, which threw down a marine. Another volley crashed from the gate and two other marines were plucked backwards, one spinning over the walkway and down into the dried out moat. A ball scored Corporal Forge's left cheek, exposing his back teeth.

Kennedy halted his men thirty paces from the gate and the platoon hammered a volley into the Frenchmen.

'Advance!' he ordered, and they pressed on through their own powder smoke. Behind him, Gamble and the remaining redcoats closed the gap, still carrying the ladders. 'Halt!' The men were below the main gate's walls now so were safe from above. 'Load!'

They ran the ladders up against the shoulders of the curtain wall and the first men began to climb. Gamble pushed past the ranks to steer the third ladder against the wall. A musket fired through the portcullis and the ball tore a rent in his sleeve. He pushed men to the rungs. The marines fired another volley and the defenders twitched and died against the metal rods. The first seamen arrived, and they charged with boarding pikes and the wicked blades ripped into torsos, throats and legs.

'Push!' Pym was shouting. A seaman next to him was shot in the face and it seemed to him that the man's head just disappeared in an explosion of blood. 'Push the bastards!' He slashed his sabre at a Frenchman, trying to stab him with his bayonet, and put his pistol to the man's chest and pulled the trigger. Blood misted the tight space. The enemy hung against the bars, kept upright by the press of men from behind. A sword sliced and another musket spurted flame through the churning rill of smoke to send another Jack Tar to his grave, but the landing party was winning this fight.

'Up! Up! Up!' Gamble shouted as some of the men started to look for cover. A marine staggered. Sergeant Powell kicked a man who hung back. They could not falter now for it would weaken the attack. Every man had to climb, not knowing if the next second would be his last. The only way to survive horror was to win. Gamble saw Willoughby and Crouch at the rear and ran over to them, thrusting them towards the ladders. 'Get up there!' he snarled.

Crouch looked terrified, but they both climbed. Men scrambled up the rungs, but then a marine was hit by a shot from the flanking battery to the left. He slipped and toppled to the moat, body twisting as he screamed. More jostled to climb the ladders. Sailors waited the rear, all armed with cutlasses, muskets, dirks and pistols.

'Up! Faster!' Gamble bellowed for the line seemed to falter. He saw Kennedy about to scale a ladder, sword in one hand which would make the climb awkward. 'Harry!' he called. 'Bring your sword to bear at the top!' Kennedy understood and rammed his weapon home.

The marines climbed with their bayonet-tipped muskets slung over their shoulders. A redcoat slipped half-way up and knocked the five below him to the ground. They cursed him and picked themselves up to continue.

The defender's fire was continuous, a staccato drum beat of musketry, but Gamble could tell the walls weren't fully manned. He had expected larger volleys. Grech had said that the French numbered perhaps three hundred, but experience told him that perhaps a hundred were defending the fort. If that was the case, where was the rest?

His legs burned with the effort of the climb. Gun smoke roiled thick from the ramparts and shots echoed about him. He couldn't see the enemy; his world was a pair of dirty white legs, a ladder and a limestone wall. Steel crashed against steel. Bullets flayed flesh. A man called out in English for his mother. Gamble coughed from the acrid stink. Then Crouch, with his bandaged hand, disappeared, and Gamble knew he had reached the top. He unsheathed his sword and threaded through an embrasure to drop down onto the parapet.

Bright blood spotted the stone. Marsh lay dying next to a fusilier and Gamble stepped over them, slipping in glistening gore. A grenadier was cocking his musket. Gamble levelled his pistol and the shot dissolved the man's face in blood. To his right, the defenders blasted the walls from the central St Paul's Bastion, while to the left, French crowded the Notre Dame Bastion. A ragged line of musket-armed French spat malice from the courtyard, but their aim was put off by the group of seamen who still poured fire from the portcullis. The parapets were filling with marines and the seamen swarmed the ladders skilfully as though they were climbing ships' rigging.

'My platoon to me!' Gamble pushed men aside as he went right. A hail of musketry tore scraps of stone from the stonework as he ran. A ball snatched at his bicorn, turning it.

An enemy swung his musket like a club. Gamble ducked and unceremoniously tipped him over the side of the parapet, hearing his cries all the way down. A bayonet lunged and Gamble battered it aside with his straight-bladed cutlass. The steel clanged, sending sparks over the body of a dead defender who had been shot through an eye. The blackened wound still smouldered. Gamble kicked his assailant, punched and grabbed the musket's hot barrel, turning it to the left with all his strength. His fingers burned, but the Frenchman could not bring his weapon back and gave a high pitched scream as the long cutlass cut him through shoulder to breastbone.

'Kill the bastards!' Powell bellowed.

Pace shot a man less than three feet away in the face. A grenadier, with huge arms and a long flowing moustache, fired his musket but the ball went wide. Gamble rammed his sword at his face, and the enemy dropped his weapon to claw at the ugly blade. Gamble withdrew it and the man hissed, but held on tightly, as blood dripped from his cut fingers.

A long bayonet stabbed the air and Gamble stumbled backwards with the muscled enemy on top of him. His hands were locked with the weight of the grenadier's body, as heavy as solid iron. The Frenchman tried to bite his face with crooked yellow teeth, snapping from underneath the moustache. Another two enemies appeared above. One went to stab Gamble in the face with his bayonet when a musket ball drummed into his chest to throw him backwards. The grenadier managed to get a bloodied hand free and tried to find purchase around Gamble's throat, but Gamble jerked his head and the moustached man couldn't get a grip.

A marine, shouting something incomprehensible, stabbed the other defender in the throat with the spike atop an axe head and swung another onto the grenadier's head. The sharp steel cleaved through black hair with a wet crack. The Frenchman's grip immediately eased, and his eyes rolled up into his skull. Gamble threw off the body and Powell hauled him upright.

'Thank you, Archie,' Gamble said. 'Now let's tear them to shreds!'

The defenders retreated, but in good order. A musket flamed and a ball shattered a marine's collar bone, spinning him around. The soldiers screamed terrible battle-cries as they began their grim job of clearing the defenders off the parapet with quick professional close-quarter work. Gamble trod on a fallen ramrod and his boots crunched on burnt wadding. The French reached steps and began descending into the bastion.

'Bayonets!' Powell bellowed. 'I want bayonets!'

'Charge the bastards!' Gamble screamed, blinking another man's blood from his eyes. There was no drum to beat the order, but the marines and Jack Tars surged forward.

'*Tirez!*' The French had been waiting, and their muskets jerked a handful of attackers backwards. Their officer, dressed in a patched brown coat, was horrified to see the savage-looking men advance unperturbed by the musketry. His men were mostly conscripts and they had fired too high. Now they had only steel bayonets with which to defend themselves.

'Get in close, boys!' Powell ordered. 'A Shawnee Indian named Blue Jacket once told me that a naked woman stirs a man's blood, but a naked blade stirs his soul. So go in with the steel. Lunge! Recover! Stance!'

'Charge!' Gamble turned the order into a long, guttural yell of defiance.

Those redcoats and seamen, with loaded weapons discharged them at the press of the defenders, and a man in the front rank went down with a dark hole in his forehead. Gamble saw the officer aim a pistol at him. A wounded Frenchman, half-crawling, tried to stab with his *sabre-briquet*, but Gamble kicked him in the face. He dashed forward, sword held low. The officer pulled the trigger, the weapon tugged the man's arm to his right, and the ball buzzed past Gamble's mangled ear as he jumped down into the gap made by the marines' charge. A French corporal, wearing a straw hat, drove his bayonet at Gamble's belly, but he dodged to one side and rammed his bar-hilt into the man's dark eyes.

'Lunge! Recover! Stance!'

Wet blades made quick work and the bastion was awash with blood and mangled bodies. A redcoat kneed a defender in the groin and clasped his hands over his face, thumbs digging into eye-sockets. The men with boarding pikes thrust them at faces, quick jabs, one after the other, driving the enemy down where bayonets could kill them. Men grunted, shouted and cursed. A musket flamed, so close that the orange tongue touched a Frenchman's chest as Willoughby shot him through the body. The huge marine barged past the falling enemy and stabbed with his bayonet at the French officer. The man slashed at the steel with his thin sword, ducked another of the marines' assault, but a boarding pike took him in the throat and he quivered like a landed fish. His head flopped back as he buckled to his knees. Willoughby kicked the body backwards.

'Crouch is dead, sir,' he said, over his shoulder. 'Caught a Frenchie ball between the eyes.'

Gamble didn't know what to say to that. Willoughby had not turned to face him and Gamble somehow felt he was entirely to blame. The marine had been trouble and he had wished him dead many times, but he had died doing his duty, and that was all that would be remembered of him. Now was not the time to dwell on such things.

'Remember Acre!' he screamed. A marine next to him collapsed, holding his stomach, dark blood oozing between his fingers. 'Charge! Charge!'

The blades had done their work, they had carved their way across the parapet and the tight-packed French ranks had been destroyed. His men had done it!

'Cannon!' A voice called and Gamble turned, horrified, to see the French had brought artillery onto the southern ramparts. A gun captain, seeing that the enemy had concentrated the attack on the doomed St Paul's Bastion, raised his sword to signal the attack.

*

St Paul's Bastion had been taken, but the fort had not yet fallen. The attackers clogged the blood drenched parapet above the main gate, but they still had not taken St Anthony's Bastion or the Notre Dame Bastion.

Tessier's men were fighting hard, shocked by the attack, but were offering a stubborn defiance. Tessier formed a thin line of sixty men across the courtyard and gunners ran to the seaward facing gun batteries to turn them on the redcoats. If they timed it right, and aimed true, the gun salvoes could win this battle.

Musket balls hissed about him. A sergeant was shot through the head at his side, and two more were maimed by the English sailors at the main gate, but Tessier's life seemed charmed and he remained unscathed. He picked up a fallen musket and shot a redcoat dead. His men fired up at the walls and bullets pockmarked the stone. Thirty had been hauled from the hospital and given muskets to fire. A dozen inside barricaded the building and offered the attackers another obstacle.

'Keep firing!' Tessier ordered. Blood splattered his blue coat, but none of it was his. He lived and grinned because the guns would soon shatter the red devils at the wall and Dominance would be riven to spatters of gore. France would win today and the enemy would bleed out their lives. His men just needed to hold their positions for a little while longer. 'Keep firing! Keep firing! Keep fir - ' Tessier's voice was suddenly drowned out as the whole world exploded in thunder, fire and dust.

*

'There's the Prince of Waves!' Gamble shouted and the men cheered.

The *Sea Prince* had sailed around Comino in the night, hidden by its great island cliffs, then sailed in the pre-dawn light to anchor facing the harbour of Mġarr. It had come to rest with its port broadside facing the fort, and had just silenced the French seaward guns with an ear-splitting salvo at the north-facing batteries. The cannons had been fired by masterful gunners, and Gamble could see all that was left of them were smoking pits of twisted metal and gore. A gust of scorching air blew over the fighting men, and scraps of stone rained down like a mighty hailstorm.

Only the Notre Dame Bastion remained to be taken and the fort would be theirs. Gamble turned back across the outer defences to see scores of Gozitans swarming across the bridges to the ladders.

He could see Zeppi waving a black flag showing a white Maltese cross, shouting encouragement and death to the French. Marines had reached the flanking battery. The gun team went down under blades, but not without a fight. A marine was hit in the chest with a gunner's rammer and disappeared over the wall. One of Kennedy's men stepped forward and shot the Frenchman dead.

Gamble drew a sleeve across his forehead, mixing black powder, sweat and blood. The French troops had formed a line across the courtyard, but were now unable to concentrate because of the devastating cannonade at their rear. There was not a moment to lose if Gamble was to consolidate his victory. Then, he saw Tessier, sword bright in his hand, and he clenched his jaw.

The marines and landing party charged down to capture St Anthony's Bastion. Gamble and Sergeant Powell ran back along the parapet, across the gatehouse to the Notre Dame Bastion. Sand and weed strewn stone stairs led down the courtyard where Gamble would find and kill the Frenchman.

The parapets were thickening with Gozitans, marines and sailors. Gamble pushed past men, keen for revenge. He almost slipped on gore-covered bottom steps where one of his men lay dead, his brains splattered like spilled porridge. A callow-faced *chasseur* with blood oozing from his mouth aimed his musket, and Gamble shoved Powell aside as the ball smacked into the stonework beside him. The defender lunged his bayonet at Gamble who, with a well-practised reflex, dodged, tripped the man, and then chopped down through his windpipe. Two men came out of the nearest building which was the chapel dedicated to the Blessed Virgin Mary of Graces. Powell brought his musketoon to bear and the defenders were blasted backwards in an explosion of misting blood.

'Jesus, but I could do with a drink.' Powell wiped his mouth, his eyes searching for more enemies as he loaded.

'We'll drink ourselves stupid tonight,' Gamble said.

'Amen to that, sir.'

'There's bound to be plenty of wine.'

'I would prefer rum or a nice pint of beer, sir,' Powell said over a musket ball hitting the wall with a loud crack above him. 'They used to serve rare stuff at The Turk's Head.'

'I remember the brawls too, Archie,' Gamble said of the particular Plymouth inn. 'You never lost a fight, did you?'

The sergeant chuckled reminiscently. 'No, sir. And I won't be losing this one either.'

Pym's men had raised the portcullis and suddenly the defenders were being pushed back to the middle of the huge courtyard. Rooke had been shot in the shoulder, but waved the men on, regardless.

'Ben! Raise the flag!' Gamble shouted. Pym cut the halyard that held the Tricolour above the main gate and ran the Union Flag up it. Gamble watched it with pride. It had been the bundle that he had asked his friend to bring. It would show that the fort had fallen to Grech's men, the islanders, and most importantly, to the *Sea Prince*.

'Where did the bugger go, sir?' Powell said, watching the defenders throwing down their weapons and the officers begging the redcoats for protection before the Gozitans got there.

Voices cheered the raising of the Union Flag. The ripple of voices echoed across the battlements as the final shots rang out.

'I can't see the bastard,' Gamble's throat was parched and his voice cracked as he spoke over the noise. The stench of sizzling flesh coming from the destroyed batteries was overpowering. The air was filled with drifting patches of acrid smoke.

'Sir! We've won! We gave Johnny Crapaud a proper drubbing!' Kennedy shouted. He was red-faced, coated with grime, but exultant.

Gamble thumped his arm. 'I'm glad to see you, Harry,' he said, pleased to find his friend alive. 'You did well back there.'

'Coming from you, sir,' Kennedy said, 'that is a compliment in itself.' He gazed back at the battlements. 'My word, what an achievement to tell!'

Gamble's throat was raw, frayed and he had to swill out his dry mouth with brackish wine from his canteen before being able to speak again. He hawked and spat. 'Have you seen Tessier?'

'No, sir.'

'He's here somewhere. I want all our NCOs looking too. I'll ask Pym for help. Check the prisoners first and remember we must be quick! I don't want the bastard getting away!'

'He won't, sir!'

The men inside the barracks and hospital decided to surrender rather than prolong the fight. Marines, under a bandaged Corporal Forge, brought those who were not too ill outside and stationed guards at the doors. Pace and two others helped the wounded move to the hospital where they would be treated. Some would not survive the night. Men with their bone-dry throats, slaked their thirst from their canteens, or from those of the dead. Others went to look for the fresh water wells.

There is nowhere for Tessier to go, Gamble contemplated. He looked at faces, unknown, bloody, grim and sooty with powder. Water and wine was passed around. A man crawled with a trail of blood dripping from his mouth. The unwounded gathered in the centre, weapons discarded, a grisly remnant of the garrison. Men of the same height and build as Tessier were scrutinized, but eye colour, hair and features didn't match. Powell and Kennedy returned.

'No sign of him,' Kennedy said, exasperated. 'Perhaps he was killed by the ship's barrage?'

'No,' Gamble replied feverishly, 'I saw him here.' The bastard was dangerous and clever, but not as much as Gamble. 'We search the living and then we search the dead. We search the rooms again. I want the wounded looked at. Kitchens, storerooms, the chapel…'

The prospect of prolonging the search made Kennedy's exhausted face lengthen.

Gamble saw it and tilted his head. 'What is it?'

Kennedy sighed. 'We have no guarantee that he's still alive. We could both die looking for him.'

Gamble's eyes darkened. 'I want him found.'

'So do I,' Kennedy said, 'but . . .'

'What?'

'To what end will this accomplish?'

Gamble was also fatigued, bruised and his fingers throbbed from touching the hot musket barrel, but Sam's murderer had to be found.

'It's our duty to avenge a fallen brother,' Gamble said, glowering.

Kennedy's eyes twitched. 'You do not understand, sir. Sam is not - '

'Samuel Riding-Smyth is not Robert Carstairs. And both are now dead.' Gamble was angry, but let it pass. He clasped Kennedy's forearm. 'I know. I do understand. But it's something I have to do.'

Kennedy understood the torment of losing both friends, and so nodded. 'Then let's find the bastard and bury him.'

Gamble smiled and shook his arm in gratitude.

The buildings were combed, even the cemetery. Gamble resorted to naming him in the hope that one of his countrymen might give him away, but those that knew him had not seen him. A middle-aged French officer was brought to Gamble, Kennedy and Pym.

'I am *Général* Évrard Chasse, the commander of this garrison,' the Frenchman said haughtily, but in good English.

'Captain Gamble, sir.'

'How did you find the British greeting this morning, sir?' Pym asked, with much intended impertinence. 'You should have just left the door open, old boy.'

Chasse grunted. He turned away from the smirking Pym to face Gamble. 'Are you the senior ranking officer here?'

'I am, sir.'

'I'm to negotiate terms with a captain,' Chasse sounded aghast. He brought out a large handkerchief and placed it against his face. The smell of open bowels and the copper stink of blood flayed his delicate nostrils.

'No, sir,' Gamble said respectfully. 'I'm to escort you to Captain Eaton of His Majesty's *Sea Prince*, where you will discuss terms.'

Chasse gazed at the marines who were tending to his wounded soldiers. He suddenly felt rather humbled. He cleared his throat. 'I understand you have been asking about *Capitaine* Tessier?'

'I'm interested in acquiring the bastard, sir.'

'Are you the marine officer that ambushed him?'

'I am.'

Chasse's eyes narrowed at the recognition. 'I understand the fight hurt him more than any bullet or blade, *Capitaine* Gamble. He told me he had escaped his bonds and brought news of your arrival. I must confess I ignored him. I never liked him from the start. Perhaps if I'd listened to him, then you would not be here, and I would still have a garrison.'

Gamble smiled. 'I would have still beaten you, sir.'

Chasse pursed his lips and allowed a smile to touch them. '*Bon*. I wish I could help you with his capture. You seem awfully keen to acquire him?'

'He murdered my second lieutenant, sir,' Gamble said and the *général's* bearded mouth immediately lolled open.

'*Mon Dieu!*'

'I allowed Tessier to keep his sword and he murdered my officer and fled,' Gamble said. 'I will hunt him even if it takes me to the gates of Hell.'

'He made no mention of this to me. I expect my men to be honourable, even in defeat. Chivalry still exists in France. That was an act of cold-blooded murder.' He swore and leaned closer to

Gamble. 'We are enemies, but I hope you find him, *Capitaine*. I really hope you do.'

'I will, sir.'

'*Bon*. I trust you will allow our garrison surgeon Vipond to stay? He is very able and will treat even the locals.' Chasse sniffed to show that he found that somewhat distasteful.

'Thank you, sir.'

Gamble left to check the outer walls, the destroyed batteries, the Guardian Angel Bastion which contained a stone powder store with a conical roof and a five-sided watchtower. The walls offered good defence, for most had firing platforms and loopholes to allow musketry, but the French had capitulated and no one remained there. Gamble walked to the watchtower overlooking the sea. The *Sea Prince* was still at anchor and to the east, the waters were dotted with fishing craft outside the harbour. Gulls circled high in the air. There was no one below on the cliffs and rocky shoreline.

Triumph was his and somehow he was unable to feel the elation of it. He slammed a palm into the stone in frustration and turned around to find Kennedy waiting at the foot of the watchtower. He looked grim.

'Tessier?'

'I think you'd better come down, sir,' he said. 'We've found something.'

They had won, men had died, but by God's grace, they had won. And whether Grech was right about winning a victory for God or not, Gamble swore, because Tessier had gone and none of this mattered one bit.

*

God damn all Englishman, Tessier cursed.

They had taken the fort effortlessly and all *la chatte* could do was to surrender. I bet he never drew his blade, or fired his pistol. The yellow coward! Tessier had watched the general from the Guardian Angel Bastion, knowing that as soon as the English flag was raised, then the war ship would not fire for fear of hitting their own men. The attackers swarmed into the buildings and Tessier saw Gamble hunting for him. Whilst the prisoners lay down their weapons, Tessier had crept under the shadowed wall to where a narrow set of stairs led down to the sally-port. The winch system holding the portcullis was rusty, but with enough effort the bars raised to allow a single man to escape outside at a time. He had been the first out and a few of the garrison had seen him escape and now a slow trickle of men stumbled in the morning light. All of them went west, but Tessier, a survivor, knew the most dangerous route was the only way to freedom.

*

Nine months later on the morning of 8th September, 1800, Captain Simon Gamble looked up at Valletta's ancient gates and sighed heavily.

Malta's capital city had remained all this time in French hands. It was the only foothold the enemy still had, but today at midday, the garrison would march out with the honours of war, and the country would pass to the British.

But there was one man inside who had no such morality or virtue as far as Gamble was concerned.

After Fort Dominance had fallen, half-hidden near the wreckage of the seaward batteries, Kennedy had discovered the sally-port. Gamble had climbed down there. Gozitans had caught ten men outside in the hills, but none of them was Tessier. He took a score of his battle-weary marines down the cliffs to the water's edge, scouring every rock and bush, and down into the port of Mġarr. By the next sunrise, Tessier was still missing and Gamble came to the conclusion that Frenchman would have tried to reach the final French held bastion: Valletta. It was where Gamble would have gone.

Upon landing in St Paul's Bay, Gamble had Tessier's name, rank and a sketch of him posted and distributed throughout the Maltese suburbs in case he had not reached the safety of the gates. Gamble had even offered a reward out of his own money, but no one had seen him and Tessier remained gallingly at large. Kennedy had voiced that he had been wounded in the attack and had died, or most possibly drowned crossing the sea, but Gamble refused to believe that explanation.

The French ship, *Guillaume Tell*, had sneaked out of the harbour during the spring in an attempt to break through the British naval blockade, but had been captured early the next morning. Gamble had hoped Tessier was on-board and had been allowed access on board. One Frenchman knew a Tessier, but he had been killed the battle of Arcole. Apart from discovering three British deserters, the captain was not present and he resumed his search for him in the city.

The sun was bright and Gamble had not known an autumn sun so powerful or felt so very hot. Sweat trickled down his back. *Perhaps I'm not well*, he thought. He'd not be eating very much lately, or sleeping and Powell had shown concern. He knew he had become obsessed with capturing Sam's killer, and until now, he could do nothing but sit and wait.

The marines and a regiment of newly formed Maltese soldiers would be the first to enter the city after the enemy had marched out. The Maltese Light Infantry with their blue coats faced red and black hats styled with a green plume waited with nervous expectation. And it was an anxious time. They had families, friends and relatives inside the city and the last few months of the blockade had been incredibly desperate. The city folk and the garrison had eaten every horse, pack animal, fowl, rabbit, dog, cat and rat that they could to ward off starvation. The cisterns had long been emptied, the granaries were bare and even a frigate had been broken up for firewood. Disease had claimed hundreds of lives. Valletta, the most humble of cities, was a vision of Hell on Earth.

'They'll fly like bleeding sparrows the moment we march in,' Bray said sneeringly of the new regiment. 'They're not proper soldiers.'

'Quiet in the ranks,' Sergeant Powell called out.

'A bad omen having foreigners in British pay,' Bray muttered despite the warning, digging a dirty finger around a nostril and pulling out something foul and glistening. 'Especially from this shit-hole of a country. Cowards, the bleeding lot of them. Left it late to enter the fort, didn't they? We lost some good men there.'

'A pity you can't claim to be amongst them then, Bray,' Gamble said, walking down the depleted ranks.

There were just twenty men present. The marines had lost a total of eighteen in the attack, and the rest of the company were recovering from a fever that had swept through the island in the summer like wildfire. The main hospital, the *Santa Infermeria*, with its precious medicines, was in French hands and Kennedy, one of the affected, lay in one of the temporary hospitals set up in a church. Zeppi still lived and had returned to his home in Mdina, the ancient walled city that had once been the island's capital, to assist with the rebuilding of destroyed homes.

'That's unfair, sir,' Bray wailed. 'I did my duty. I earn my tuppence a day.'

'Keep your assumptions to yourself, Bray,' Powell said. 'It's too early in the day for your bullshit.'

You shall pay life for life, the voice said in Gamble's head. He gazed up at the gulls that circled the city's walls like vultures. Behind him, men of the 30th and the 89th Foot stood in line. Maltese folk watched from doors and windows. The smell of the sea was as powerful as the pervasive stink of sewage.

Gamble had been given a presentation sword in honour of the fort's capture. Pym had said Captain Eaton was going to give a generous amount to the officers for their efforts, but prize money could take ages to come through and, once the Admiralty and the lawyers had taken their share, there would be little left. Gamble could not wait for the money, no matter how much, and had pawned his presentation sword. It had fetched eight pounds and he had sent the money home to his mother to help with the debt. There was still a huge amount to pay, but Gamble vowed that he would not stop until he did. He felt a catch in his throat as he thought of his family's plight.

It was time. He could sense it.

Gamble's neck muscles tensed when he heard the first notes of music. The French were playing *la Marseillaise*, the Revolutionary anthem. The gates juddered and opened slowly and Gamble automatically wondered whether Tessier would be the first to march out. French soldiers shouldered their muskets. Drums and flutes played and the first French troops marched out with their flags held high under a brilliant sun.

They had not eaten for days; their uniforms hung ragged and loose. However, they had done their best to smarten up their clothes. Rents were stitched up, boots, belts, buttons and badges had been polished, jackets brushed and hair, moustaches and beards had been trimmed. Some had yellow skin and most had lost teeth, but they marched with a cocksure swagger. Transport ships waited in the harbour for them to embark quickly because the British didn't want the responsibility of feeding them.

Gamble watched as Major-General Henry Pigot and a knot of other high-ranking officers saluted the enemy smartly as they passed by. The civilians had been kept back by the British regiments, but it didn't stop a few from launching scraps of rotten food or stones at the French over their heads.

'Bloody children!' Adams said in exasperation. 'Look at 'em!'

'Just conscripts,' Gamble suggested, noticing that some were indeed absurdly youthful.

'Hey, Adder,' Bray said, pointing with what could amount to a chin to a marching individual who was oblivious to the scrutiny, 'that one there is still wearing his pudding cap!' Adams and the men laughed rowdily. Toddlers wore a thick padding around the waist called a 'pudding', meant to protect them should they tumble while learning to walk. They also wore a protective helmet called a pudding cap. 'Go back to your mother's skirts!'

'How the hell did these milksops terrify Europe, sir?' Powell commented, face glistening with sweat.

'Aye, they look like dirty-looking weans not soldiers,' Corporal MacKay said over more jeering.

But Gamble wasn't listening. He walked forward, his eyes regarded the scores of faces that charily marched past. It was an endless task. Unfamiliar face after unfamiliar face blurred past, but none were Tessier. He shouted out the name, but although enemy faces watched him, none responded. Frustration tugged his conscience and instead of waiting, he walked up to the gates, and sprinted inside.

'Sir?' Powell anxiously called after him. 'Sir!'

Gamble heard other voices call him back, most notably from Brigadier-General Moncrieff, who commanded the Maltese Light Infantry. He wanted Tessier. Damn their eyes! Couldn't they understand? Sam's murderer was inside!

The streets were empty except for the long column of marching French. The air was cloyed with the smell of death and decay. Nothing else moved.

'Jean Tessier!' Gamble bellowed, hatred etched on his face. The tiredness and maddening inactivity of the past few months were instantly forgotten. 'I know you're here! You hook-nosed, cowardly, son of a bitch! Show yourself!'

Suspicious eyes regarded him, and unknown voices cursed and jeered his appearance. He watched as hope for revenge began to dissipate like mist burning away under a morning sun. Goddamn the bastard! He had to be here! He had to!

Tears pricked Gamble's eyes at the thought of never catching the killer. The rank memory of it had festered like a battle wound. He had been put forward by Eaton to command the new Maltese regiment, but in the last few months he had trouble sleeping and focusing on his duties. Powell had found him wandering the streets one morning unable to fathom how he had got there. It was not all down to drink. Vengeance had consumed Gamble so badly that the command had passed over to Captain of Marines James Weir, from the *Audacious*. But Gamble didn't care about reputation and less about honour.

He wanted revenge.

His eyes, flicked up the column, and one of the Frenchmen hung back, causing a disturbance in the files. He was two hundred yards away, and although much thinner, there was no mistaking who it was.

Both men stared at each other.

Gamble's mouth twitched. 'Tessier!' he suddenly roared, and charged forward.

The Frenchman twisted to his right, fleeing down a shit-reeking alley where sullen, hollowed out faces watched from partially opened windows. Tessier had taken a risk by fleeing into the city burning with hatred for France, but he was desperate and desperate men will do anything to survive.

Gamble's boots thumped on the cobbles and he turned into the alley. A pistol flashed from the shadows; the ball shattered stone to his left, driving shards into his cheek. Gamble ran on, not caring if the Frenchman had another pistol, or not.

Ragged washing hung between the tall narrow buildings. No one could use a carriage here. Two beggars, huddled beneath filthy blankets slept on wide steps. Gamble ran past a group of children who looked like half-dressed skeletons. Starvation and poverty ruled these streets. Foul liquid squelched underfoot and tall weeds climbed up pillared doorways. He ran on, chasing the disappearing form of Tessier, heading further into the labyrinthine lanes, Gamble realised he was lost. The heat smothered the still air. He passed his hand across his sweat-laced face. Alleys became yet more alleys, and he could not see where the enemy had gone. Damn! He would not lose the bastard for the third time! He chose the darkest path simply because he assumed the Frenchman would seek out substantial cover. He saw shadows move, ducked behind a squat barrel covered in mould, drew his pistol and cocked it. He edged beside the wall and heard a murmur. Gamble peered around the corner to see a bone-thin whore at work with her mouth and nothing more. He ran on ahead. More tight corners, and then two gaunt-looking men blocked his way.

'A Frenchman!' Gamble told them. 'He ran into these alleys. Have you seen him?'

The tallest one, a rakish fellow that reminded Gamble of Adams, turned to his companion, dipped his head and beckoned for Gamble to follow. They turned left, crossed a garden bereft of fruit and vegetables, past a series of empty poultry coops, down a series of steps to a grand sixteenth century Baroque piazza. The facades of the buildings were designed so that light and shadow created dramatic effects as it playfully spread over the city. And despite the siege, the buildings here looked pristine and flowers grew up the balconies and flourished at the windows. The men grinned with yellowed teeth and pointed straight ahead. He thanked them before sprinting down the cobbles towards the harbour.

*

He had panicked.

Tessier cursed his own stupidity. He should have remained in the column where he would have been protected by his compatriots. Instead, he saw an enemy coming for him like a revenant rising from a dark tomb, and he had run away like a coward.

Except this was no longer a French stronghold. The forts had all been captured and surrendered and the glorious revolutionary soldiers had been defeated. If the supply ships had made it through the blockade, Vaubois might still have been able to defend the city, but with no food, limited ammunition and disease rampant, defeat was inevitable.

Tessier remembered the gut-wrenching escape from Fort Dominance where villagers spat at him and threw rocks. One man had brought out a pistol and the ball had slapped the air as it passed his face. Another man had chased him with an ancient boar spear and Tessier, exhausted from the tussle, had jumped into the water. He had nearly drowned in that cold grey sea, only just managing to cling to a rock whilst the enemy searched the shoreline. The English warship was anchored outside the village, and although Tessier could see men on-board, no one had spotted him. Hours passed by. Then, when he considered it was clear, he swam ashore to hide in the malodorous marshland outside Mġarr. His body shivered violently and his skin was blue and wrinkled like withered fruit, but in the night-dark light he lived. He had crept to a fishing boat, donned a salt-stained boat cloak and rowed out to Malta's monochrome coastline. He had somehow managed to escape capture by abandoning the boat to swim into the harbour. From there, it had been easy to climb the city walls and to safety.

He had written his account of the marines ambush, the fort's surrender and his opinion of Chasse, to Vaubois. Tessier wanted Gamble cashiered and Vaubois promised to take his complaint to the senior English officer when he was in a position to. Weeks went past. Months. A burning hunger for revenge changed to a desire for provisions. And until today, Tessier reflected that he would never see Gamble again.

Sunlight twinkled on the water, dazzling like a million diamonds scattered across its surface.

Tessier loaded his pistol in the shadows where the air was still and cool. He had two of them, a knife and a sword, and, although starving and crippled with stomach cramps, he would fight as he always did

With everything he had.

*

Gamble could not see the Frenchman.

You shall pay life for life . . .

Gamble ran out of cover, but no shot assailed him.

Wind tugged the aroma of seaweed and shellfish from the sea into the streets. The roads zigzagged down to the deserted wharves. Waves crashed against the breakwater. Three French warships were docked, blockaded by the British in the harbour. They stood empty and forlorn with a smattering of merchant ships and smaller vessels. Wicker baskets, nets and hauling ropes were stacked up and tiny fishing boats and skiffs bobbed on the water. The Maltese were at work, allowed to fish the shallow waters. The womenfolk in thick skirts combed the quays for crabs, lobsters and clams. His eyes darted along road, up to the vast walls and down to where towering buildings gleamed gold and palm trees added to the exotic curiosity of the island.

A pistol banged from the shoreline and Gamble impulsively ducked. The ball plucked at his temple, scoring a slash by his right eye. He was dazed, but not disabled. Sea birds screamed at the noise that pounded across the water.

You shall pay life for life...

Gamble, feeling warm liquid dripping into his ear, brought up his pistol, and pulled the trigger. He knew it had gone high and was surprised to see Tessier stumble, clutching his head, blood rushing through fingers. Gamble jumped off the winding weed-strewn road, and unsheathed his sword. The blade flashed silver as it roared free of its scabbard in the quest for blood. The French captain managed to bring a second pistol to bear and Gamble saw the black muzzle. It was too late to get out of the way. The air burst with flame and smoke and noise. Gamble's right thigh felt as though it had been hit with a hammer, followed by pain that seared white-hot. His leg buckled and he skidded across the ground.

Tessier, blood running down his face, dropped the pistol and reached for his sword when black spots flashed in front of his eyes. He staggered, slipped and tumbled rearward onto algae-flecked rocks. Seawater and blood stung his eyes. He was blinded and he awkwardly pulled his slim sword free, slashing the air with wild strokes, suspecting Gamble was upon him.

But Gamble was still on his side, blood oozing from the wound. He undid his sash and tied it around his thigh. He felt light-headed; blood was crusting at his temple as he hobbled to where the stinking water lapped against the rocks.

Tessier scooped water onto his face, clearing his eyes to see a red hunter stalk above. He shook his head and droplets of bright blood pitted the water's surface.

'Get up, you coward!' Gamble bellowed and spat. 'You have no honour!'

Tessier felt like a cornered beast, the pain in his head threatening to split his skull in two, but his senses were still wickedly sharp. He brought his sabre up.

'You devil! You allowed your cutthroats to slaughter my men,' Tessier replied in French, oblivious to what Gamble had said. Blood and seawater matted his head and dripped from his chin. He wiped his face with a sleeve. 'You English are a disease! A pox on you!'

Gamble spat to show whatever Tessier had said meant nothing. He was no warrior of finesse. He fought without the airs and graces learned at the fencing schools; he learned his skill from battles. His cutlass was intended for cleaving rather than duelling. It was a bone-breaker, a flesh-cutter, and a killer. He thrust it at Tessier's tanned face, who swept it away with practised ease. Tessier slashed the air between the two of them in a series of lightning arcs that threatened to smash through Gamble's inelegant defences. Gamble, pain shooting down his leg, barely had enough time to react, recoiling and parrying. Both men were of the same height, but Gamble was bigger and Tessier knew it would be skill that would win. The Frenchman twisted, slipped and blocked a low strike that might have disembowelled him, but his sabre was no match for the solid weight of Gamble's ugly blade and he was fast losing strength.

Shouts came from the streets and redcoats were clambering down the steep steps and cobbled roads to where they fought. A score of Maltese, drawn by the sounds of pistol fire, watched the fight with nervous intrigue.

Gamble kicked with his good leg, but his wound exploded in agony and so the attack lumbered. Tessier sliced, but Gamble was already stepping away. Blood was filling his right boot. The Frenchman sprang up, and Gamble hauled his heavy sword across his body. Tessier dropped. He did not see the dirk in the scarlet-coated captain's off-hand. The curved blade easily penetrated through the flesh, sinew and muscle of his neck.

'You shall pay life, for life,' Gamble uttered, giving the weapon a savage twist, but the French captain did not understand, or would know the significance of the words.

Tessier reeled, the bone-handled dirk lodged in his neck. He made a perfunctory cut with his sword, but it was slow and clumsy. His hand dropped the sabre and reached up to pull the enemy blade free, but was too weak to do so. He tried to speak but blood filled his mouth instead.

It was all over. He knew it and as a soldier, he had to suffer a warrior's fate. But he felt at peace. Odd. Tessier barely remembered a world at peace. He had been a soldier now for over a decade. A conscript like almost everyone else, he had discovered that he liked the army, and had risen to become an officer. It brought him to adventure, to life, but he would not allow the enemy to kill him from behind, so he would face his killer like a man should do. Nevertheless, thinking of his first sea-voyage, Tessier craved to see the sea one last time.

The cutlass went through his body, driven there by a strong arm and by a hated enemy. The force was powerful enough to drive him towards the water's edge. The final ounce of breath rasped in his throat as he folded onto the blade, which Gamble still held there.

Gamble could still see the look of terror in Riding-Smyth's eyes as he lay dying.

'That's for Sam,' he said, yanking the blade free.

The French captain fell back onto the rocks below. His blood-stained hands touched the cold water. He stared up at the dazzling skyline for the last time, feeling the warmth before a black cloud misted his eyes and an eternal coldness gripped his body.

Boots pounded on the cobbles. It was Powell. 'You skewered the Frenchie proper, sir,' he said. Gamble turned and the sergeant gasped at the wounds. 'Jesus! Are you all right?'

Gamble, trembling with the exertions and despite the pain, smiled. 'Aye, Archie. I am.'

Sergeant Powell wiped sweat from his face with a red sleeve, and took hold of his officer's arm. 'Is it over now, sir? For the love of God, say it is?'

Gamble turned to stare at the corpse. Blood flowed out from the body like unravelling strands of red hair. Gulls cried overhead. 'Yes, Archie,' he said, the sun catching his ocean-blue eyes. He smiled, relief washing over him like a wave. He fought back tears, knowing that he had been narrow-minded, obstinate, selfish, and that blind anger had almost wrecked his career and ultimately his friendships. 'It's over. It's damned well over.'

A gun banged three times outside the city, a salute to the French and the start of a new chapter in Malta's history. A golden sun glowed on Valletta's domes, roofs and steeples.

It was a day in September on an island in the Mediterranean and for now the world was at peace.

HISTORICAL NOTE

Heart of Oak is a work of fiction, but nonetheless fiction grounded in fact.

Malta was a significant base in the Mediterranean that offered impressive fortifications. The French invaded on their way to Egypt in June, 1798. The islands were governed by Grand Master Hompesch who was a rather weak character, and many of the Knights of St. John were French and eager for it to be devoured by the ravenous appetite of revolutionary France.

The islands fell quickly and absolutely.

Bonaparte spent a few days on the island, establishing his headquarters at the *Palazzo Parisio*, today the Ministry of Foreign Affairs. He issued a number of social reforms based on the principles of the French Revolution, targeting social, administration, church and education.

Within three months, the Maltese revolted.

The causes of the uprising stemmed from silver taken from the Knights and from the churches and melted down to make coins. Property damaged in the invasion was not compensated, taxes rose, and there was no real freedom of the press which was owned by the government. Religious hatred also played a part.

By September the French had lost control of the countryside. With thousands of Maltese armed with muskets, pistols and agricultural tools, the troops shut themselves up in the forts and behind the city gates of Valletta. A French foraging party attacked the village of Zabbar. The plan was to encircle the village, cut it from outside help and steal as much food as they could. The French found the village completely deserted, but when they went into the narrow streets the villagers attacked them. In December, a small group of Maltese patriots in Valletta planned to open the gates to let in some two hundred armed villagers, but the vigilant French guards caught them and forty were executed by firing squad.

The Gozitans, hearing of the Maltese success, also rose up in revolt. A parish priest called Cassar was chosen as their leader and the French garrison was blocked in at the southern fort. In *Heart of Oak* I named it Dominance, but in reality the fort was named Chambray, after the Norman Count of the Order of St. John who had financed it. Negotiations between the French and Captain Ball of the Royal Navy allowed the French to evacuate the fortress and be escorted to Valletta, but only after handing over two dozen cannon, ammunition and over three thousand sacks of flour. Ball had this distributed to the islanders. No assault by British troops or Gozitans ever took place, and what is described in *Heart of Oak* is pure invention.

Over the next year the Maltese set up cannon batteries around the harbour's to stop the French from bringing in aid. They constantly skirmished with the outer forts and by the end of 1799 the first British troops had arrived: the 30th Cambridgeshire Regiment and the Irish 89th.

Fever struck. It was thought that contaminated air from the marshes at the head of the harbour was to blame and many British were affected. Malta's main hospital, the *Santa Infermeria*, was in French hands so its facilities and medicines were denied to the British and Maltese civilian population. Temporary hospitals were set up in churches. All were vastly overcrowded.

In the spring of 1800, four companies of Maltese Light Infantry were formed from local volunteers. They were led by British officers, mostly from the marines and Royal Navy, and the regiment helped harass the outer French strongholds at Cottonera and Ricasoli with notable success.

The British blockade continued to prevent French efforts to resupply the city during the early summer, and by August the situation was irrefutably desperate: no horses, pack animals, dogs, cats, fowls or rabbits still lived within the city. The cisterns had been emptied and firewood was in short supply. So serious was the need for wood that the frigate *Boudeuse*, moored in the harbour, was broken up for fuel by the beleaguered and starving garrison. Vaubois evicted several thousand Maltese from the city in the hope of rationing his remaining food. With defeat inexorable, Vaubois gave orders that the frigates *Diane* and *Justice* were to attempt a breakout for Toulon. They slipped away in the night, but were immediately spotted. *Justice* escaped and was the only French ship to do so during the blockade.

On 3rd September, with his men dying of starvation and typhus now reaching at the rate of more than a hundred men a day and with no chance of relief, Vaubois sent envoys to the British (not the Maltese) to reach terms of surrender. The victorious British and the Maltese regiment marched into Valletta on the 9th September as described in the story.

There was no HMS *Sea Prince* and yet I could not write this story without having one of the Royal Navy's ships present. I have been in awe of them since visiting HMS *Victory* at Portsmouth's Historic Dockyards as a child. I am continually amazed at the workings of the personnel, the training and professionalism that went into making Britain's fleet superior to all rivals well into the twentieth century.

The ships of the line were 'rated' according to the number of ports through which a gun could be fired. Often the number of cannon on board far exceeded the rating number. It must not be forgotten that it was the masterful command of the ships gun teams that won battles. At Trafalgar the British lost one thousand five hundred men killed or injured, whereas, the French and Spanish lost seventeen thousand! British gunnery won Trafalgar and the countless other great sea battles of the time. I have often wondered what it would have been like to walk a ship's Quarter Deck, whether sailing under a clear blue sky, or in the smoking, screaming horror of battle where sometimes the cramped fighting took place in less than the range of a pistol. Most times I am glad I am free of such experience.

Lieutenant Pym and his landing party are fictitious; however, such operations conducted on land by naval crews are not. For example, in August 1807, fifty seamen from the *Hydra* captured shore batteries whilst the rest of the crew boarded three enemy ships anchored in the harbour.

Simon Gamble is sadly an invention, but the marines were used as troops for amphibious landings as well as their duties on board the ships. A secondary duty was to suppress mutiny. There were three divisions of marines numbered 1-3, but more often they were designated by their location: Chatham, Portsmouth and Plymouth respectively. They formed part of Cavan's brigade in Sir Ralph Abercromby's Expeditionary Army that sailed to Egypt in 1801 from Malta to liberate it from French rule.

They were granted the title 'Royal Marines' in 1802 by King George III in recognition of their outstanding service.

In *Heart of Oak*, Gamble orders his men into two lines before firing a volley of musketry. It wasn't until the fighting in Spain that regulations changed from three deep to two deep lines. A three deep line was considered more solid. However, the third rank couldn't see very well and their aim was less sure, so it became two through necessity. Gamble, it seems, is a man ahead of the times.

Having Malta as a fortress island base allowed Britain to control the strategically-vital central Mediterranean. After the victories won in Egypt, Britain was supposed to leave, a condition set in the signing of the Treaty of Amiens of 1802. Tsar Alexander I was the head of the ousted Knights of St. John, and requested that it be turned over to Russian rule before agreeing any alliance with Britain. Prime Minister William Pitt the Younger categorically refused. It was Britain's refusal to comply with this clause of the treaty that was instrumental in starting the Napoleonic Wars in 1803. Malta remained in British hands until it acquired full independence in 1964.

With the capitulation of the French, Malta would resume some degree of normality. More and more British troops would land there ready for the expedition to Egypt, which meant that more battles - both land and sea - would come, and so more stories will be told.

David Cook
September, 2014
Hampshire

If you'd like to connect you can find me here at:

@davidcookauthor
www.facebook.com/davidcookauthor
http://davidcookauthor.blogspot.co.uk/
http://thewolfshead.tumblr.com

Printed in Great Britain
by Amazon

32089224R00069